Silence In Heaven

And

The Butter-Woman

And Other

Wayside Stories

TABLE OF CONTENTS

PART ONE WAYSIDE STORIES

PART TWO WAYSIDE POETRY

See our websites:

http://www.poetrybywayside.com

http://www.waysidestories.com

http://www.silenceinheavenandthebutterwoman.com

http://www.gloryworldandguiteau.com

Silence In Heaven And The Butter-Woman And Other
Wayside Stories
by Wayside

ISBN-13: 978-0615449838

ISBN-10: 0615449832

Printed in the United States of America

Made in the USA

If interested, see also the other stories and poems written by William McFarland, whose pen name was Wayside that I have now made into book form.

The story "The Glory World And Guiteau" by Wayside which is a fictional or imaginary story full of political intrigue. It talks about politics in the late 1800s and is thought provoking. This book talks of immortality and Heaven and Hell and the eternities. It is a short fictional story, political in nature about the murder and death of President Garfield along with the trial of Guiteau. There are also other short stories of political and religious themes. A sample poem, "The Machine" which is a political poem also by WAYSIDE is included in The Glory World And Guiteau. "The Glory World And Guiteau" is actually the first book out of this series while "The Silence In Heaven And The Butter-Woman And Other Wayside Stories" is actually the second book that I have made out of this series.

So who is Guiteau and who was Garfield? Please see our website at:

http://www.gloryworldandguiteau.com

The book "The Glory World And Guiteau" is part of the series of Wayside Stories by William McFarland. Said book also has many selected images from some of the old handwritten text by Wayside. Please remember these stories were actually written originally in the late 1800s by a man who was an officer in the Civil War of the United States of America and I have taken his stories and arranged them into book form. It is rare I would think that stories that were written prior to 1887 would have been kept and found later that had not previously been printed into a book. To think that this writer was writing these stories and that he was in the Civil War for the United States previously is quite something to think about. Please remember the history of these stories and poems when you read them. See our websites for details:

http://www.waysidestories.com

http://www.gloryworldandguiteau.com

More works of poetry originally written in the late 1800s by William McFarland 'Wayside' may also be found in the printed books which I have entitled, "Poetry by Wayside Book One", "Poetry By Wayside Book Two and "Poetry By Wayside Book Three." These three books are a large collection of poems that was written by William McFarland (Wayside) in the late 1800s. I have taken his poetry just as I have his old stories from his original writings and have sorted and arranged them into book form and suitable for publishing. Please remember the history of these poems when you read them and hold the books in your hands. These books of poetry are also a part of William McFarland's Wayside Stories series of books.

See our websites for details:

http://www.poetrybywayside.com

http://www.silenceinheavenandthebutterwoman.com

The photos/images after some of the short stories or poem are from the actual story or poem of which it was transcribed and typed from and are from the original handwritten manuscript of the 'Wayside' stories/letters or writings in William McFarland's book which he wrote years ago in the late 1800s. These stories and poems were separated and arranged so they would be suitable for a printed book. Some of which the actual original pages are in very poor shape and hard to read. Thus it is time for it to be printed into a book before it is lost forever. As you will notice, the handwriting is very old and as far as I can tell they were written using a quill pen. Very unusual! These stories are unique in that they were written in the 1800s! Remember the stories and poems are fictional and a product of the original writer's imagination. They are not from the thoughts or feelings of the current owner as I did not write them.

http://www.waysidestories.com

DEDICATION

This book is dedicated to my family who allowed me the time to type up these stories and poems and take photos of their pages and get them into a printed book.

This book is dedicated to my cousins that are also descendants of William McFarland so that they will be able to hold these writings of their ancestor in their hands and read the stories and poems for themselves. Now that they will be able to have their very own copies of the Wayside Stories series of books, they will as well have a family heirloom of their own in that this book is part of their family legacy as well.

In Appreciation

First I am thankful to the original writer, William McFarland, for writing these fictional stories and poems! For all his creative thoughts and his long months or years of writing these stories and poems for others to enjoy we are grateful to him. I am thankful for his incredible sense of humor and also for his political knowledge and his American pride which has brought years of joy in reading pleasure to me and I do hope it will be of enjoyment to the readers.

I am very grateful to those family members that had kept preserved and handed down and kept safe the original handwriting of William McFarland for over 100 years and had enjoyed them as I have. I am very thankful these words were not lost completely and that I found them and was the one that was given these stories and poems and was the one chosen to put these writings into book form. I only wish that William McFarland could actually see the book(s) in printed form.

I am very grateful to my family who has given me the time and had great patience and encouragement while I was reading, translating, typing, taking photos of these old papers as well as storing them and finally putting them into PDFs so they would be able to be made and published into a printed book.

FORWARD

Silence In Heaven and The Butter-Woman and Other Wayside Stories were all transcribed and typed by me from an old, handwritten book that was originally written by my ancestor, William McFarland, whose pen name was Wayside, in the late 1800s. William McFarland was my great, great, great grandpa on my father's side.

The works here as well as the images which I have taken and own were taken using my own digital camera from the actual handwritten works by my ancestor, William McFarland, (Wayside) for others to enjoy, all belong to me now as they were given to me in person from a member of my family who had treasured and protected them for years as well as other family members.

These books were handed down from one generation of my family to another for over 100 years. They were preserved and protected, enjoyed and read and stored that long. All of these relatives must have realized the worth of these stories and poems and how well they were written so they preserved them and kept them safe. To me it is a miracle to be able to publish them as this has been a goal of mine since the day I was given them.

To think I am holding the papers and the words that my great, great, great grandfather who was a Union officer in the Civil War of the United States of America had in his own hands and in his own arms and written by his own quill pen is something very special. To think these are the stories and poems that my own ancestor wrote many years ago and that while typing from these same pages that he wrote the words on, I am indeed preserving them for future generations to treasure. To think so many other relatives and ancestors also held these very papers and read the very same stories and cherished and treasured them as I have done is very special. How lucky I am to have found such a family heirloom. You will feel lucky to read these stories as well.

The images shown in this book as well as on the cover are taken from the actual handwriting of William McFarland, the original author of these writings in this book. I have made all of these book covers myself.

It was the goal of the family to have these stories and poems put into a real book and thus I am hereby doing just that. I have had these writings since 1993. I was one that was doing genealogy and had visited or called on various family members and had then found out about these stories and poems by Wayside. Fortunately for me I found the person that had these kept safe and was willing to allow me to type them up.

With the time of the internet and fast speed of the internet and home computers it is now an easier task to publish these writings into a printed book which I was told was the original author's desire.

May this printed book be an inspiration to others to do their family history and to appreciate and find their ancestors and learn of their family history. I am extremely thankful to the family members that had kept track of the names, dates and places in our family so that I was allowed to learn of them and to find these writings of Wayside as well.

Search your family and find out where you came from and what your past was. There is great joy, peace and comfort that can come from doing ones genealogy.

This book, "Silence In Heaven And The Butter-Woman Other Wayside Stories", is only a small part of a collection of Wayside's original writings which are now a series of books known as Wayside Stories.

Some of the other Wayside Stories which are stories written by Wayside are in the other story book, "The Glory World And Guiteau." This book has several fictional stories of political nature from the late 1800s. This book was also written by the same writer as this one, William McFarland (Wayside). Historians and those that adore American politics and American history should really appreciate that book. Some images of the actual old, handwriting are also included in that book as well. Actually anyone that likes things from olden times should appreciate that book.

The other books written by William McFarland 'Wayside' are a series of poetry entitled "Poetry By Wayside." This book is part of the Wayside Stories series of books by William McFarland and there are three books: Poetry By Wayside, Books One, Two and Three. It is truly a miracle these pages of poetry also have survived in the condition that they are currently in. However, the pages are old and brittle and I feel the time is now to get these into a book to preserve the poetry that Wayside wrote and probably spent years writing during his lifetime.

This book here, "Silence In Heaven And The Butter-Woman And Other Wayside Stories" consists of these stories in Part One: The Deacon's Prayer for Blaine's Sake (political), Devotion A Prayer, Moses' Obituary and Silence In Heaven and The Butter-Woman, Temperance, What Is Christianity? The Tile Setter, Gently Falls The Beautiful Snow, Prayer for the Stricken South, America, Oration 4th of July, Only A Tramp, Memorial Day, The Big Four Plus One and Ferguson. Many images of selected parts of some of these stories are being included in this book which were taken using my own digital camera. I am thankful for the wonderful software and the ability to add these images into a printed book.

William McFarland whose pen name was 'Wayside' has written a lot of poetry and a sample of these poems are in Part Two of this book, "Silence In Heaven And The Butter-Woman And Other Wayside Stories" towards the back! The poems included in this book here are: Worm Of The Still, Where There's Drink, There's Danger, In Memoriam and Gems Of The Quill and these will give the reader a sample of the fine quality of poetry which William McFarland had originally written.

Some selected photos which I have changed to black and white images from the actual original handwriting of these poems are included in this book as well for the reader to enjoy. Those that appreciate old handwriting should really enjoy these photos and appreciate them since after all they are from the late 1800s and remember these photos were taken directly from the original copies of the handwriting and some of the pages are brittle and old. The text was written directly from the originals as well.

One of William McFarland's poems, "The Machine" is in the other Wayside Stories book, "The Glory World And Guiteau." The theme on that poem is fictional and political in nature and about the same theme as the stories in the book "The Glory World And Guiteau," as it deals with politics in the late 1800s. Since that was a fictional poem about American politics that was stored in the same handwritten notebook where Wayside wrote his other stories and poems, I felt the best place for this political poem was in the fictional story book described above. The Machine was also originally written in the late 1800s and was also kept safe, preserved, hidden and protected for over 123 years by my family and myself.

The rest of the poetry written by William McFarland whose pen name was Wayside and were also written in the late 1800s are in the books, "Poetry by Wayside, Book One and Book Two." Many of the Wayside poems are also in a smaller book, which is part of "Poetry By Wayside", Book Three, Buds of Promise."

Please see my domain names/websites for more information:

http://www.poetrybywayside.com

http://www.waysidestories.com

http://www.gloryworldandguiteau.com

http://www.silenceinheavenandthebutterwoman.com

About The

Original Author

William McFarland

'Wayside'

William McFarland who wrote these works lived from 1823 to 1887. He was a real person. I am thus putting his name on these works using his pen name which was Wayside. After all, he was the one that had originally written these stories and poems. William McFarland was a Union officer in the United States Civil War. He was a school teacher as well. He was married and had three daughters as well as some grandchildren.

Now may I present yet another book from the collection of the series Wayside Stories which I have entitled, "Silence In Heaven And The Butter-Woman And Other Wayside Stories."

Who was the Butter-Woman? What happened to the Butter-Woman and why was their Silence in Heaven? What was butter doing in Heaven? Or was it heaven? It may not be about what you think it would be. This is a mystery and what a wonderful, fictional story. All of these writings and short stories are fiction. All of these stories have also been preserved, kept safe and hidden and handed down from one generation of my family to another for over 100 years. The time is NOW to have these stories shared with the general public and the best way is to have them printed into a real book or should I say a series of books.

Some of these are religious writings such as "Devotion A Prayer" and "Temperance." Some of these stories in this book are very patriotic and very American such as "America" and "Oration 4th of July" and "Prayer for the Stricken South." "The Deacon's Prayer For Blaine's Sake" is political and fictional in nature. Thus those who love American patriotism, religion and American politics should enjoy these writings.

Silence In Heaven And The Butter-Woman And Other
Wayside Stories
by Wayside

Silence In Heaven

And The Butter-Woman

Part One

Wayside Stories

By

William McFarland

Wayside

Silence In Heaven And The Butter-Woman And Other
Wayside Stories
by Wayside

CHAPTER ONE

THE DEACON'S PRAYER

FOR

BLAINE'S SAKE

BY

WILLIAM McFARLAND

'WAYSIDE'

Our, Dear, Holy Father, hear us, we pray Thee. Thy ways are above man's ways and thy thoughts past finding out. Who is able to measure arms with Thee; or, stand against the Holy One of Israel! Thou canst work and none can hinder; and no man dares to say, "Why doest thou so." The wind bloweth where it listeth. The wicked can't tell from whence it comes, nor whither it goes; but the truly loyal look with faith believing, and are admonished. But we are in a sad straight. Our enemies are as numerous as the sands of the sea and our camp is full of traitors. Our prohibitory friends who used to help us have deserted in a body and gone to running a ranch of their own. Our very doubtful friend Benjamin is very uncertain in his ways; is very tricky and hard to understand. The Green Backers laugh at our calamity and make a mock of thy Great Saint James G. Blaine. O Lord, most mighty, O Lord most powerful come to the rescue and save thine anointed; also help us to save ourselves. The waves run-over us, Selah. O Father pity us for our troubles are greater than we are able to bear. Constrain the Song of Belial and give us the Irish. Make them believe O Lord, that we shall twist the Lion's tail. Yea twist it 'till he howls. Just make them believe this 'till after the election. You very well know Oh Lord that our sympathy is not very strong. It is only their votes that we want now. After the election we shall not need them and shall cast them off because we won't need them anymore. O Father in Heaven hear us we pray Thee, and make us strong. We will all be good temperance men after the election and in off years will go it strong. But O Lord we can't do it now for we shall need all the votes we can get. Oh Lord do have mercy on us for the Germans are fast deserting to the enemy. Oh Lord help us for it is mighty hard to keep them in line 'till after the election. O Lord, would you be kind enough to stir up Conklin and have him speak for us. He is a mighty man and full of wisdom, but he sulks. We have patted him on the back, and called him "Good fellow" but he is cold and indifferent. O Lord do constrain him, turn his great wrath away; incline his heart to reason and make him help us. Do this, good, Lord, not for any worth of ours nor for the good of the party, but for Dear Blaine's sake. O, Thou, who art mighty to work and hard to handle; in mercy hear us. Confuse all our enemies and give us peace, i.e., the offices, and Thy Name shall have all the praise through Blaine. O Lord, we know that we are commanded to pray with faith believing. But, oh, Lord, our faith is weak, very weak. It is not as large as a grain of mustard seed. O mighty One increase our faith and strengthen our hold on the offices; and Thy name shall have all the praise through Blaine. O Lord, one more blessing would we ask of thy matchless power. Just give us the strength of Sampson that we may be able to twist the lion's tail 'till he yelps. We want this done for the good of the party and Blaine's sake. O Lord help us! Our exchequer is running low and we will become bankrupt if we don't get the offices. O Lord most mighty, help us now; and we will pay you back, double, after election. Yea Lord we will go farther. We will build you a house of Pearl and fill it with gold. Just give us the offices and you can have all the rest.

We are all true Native Americans, and believe that we should have all the offices i.e. those of the Blaine Stripe, O Lord hear!

We are against all foreigners especially the Catholics and Irish, but we have to bow to the necessity of the times and take them all in for Blaine's sake. These blessings and all others that we need to make the campaign a success we ask it in the name of The Machine be glory, power and Dominion forever and ever, or, as long as Blaine lives. We do thank Thee, O Lord, for Elder Ball and his famous story. Oh Lord inspire Brother Ball again and make him famous. Send one of your best lying spirits to enthuse him. We must beat this man Cleveland, or, he will beat us.

Do this for us O Lord and thy horn shall be exalted and thy name shall be great among all the people for Blaine's sake. Amen, and Amen.

Wayside

The Deacon's prayer was a clincher and called forth the loudest "Amens" all over the congregation. Indeed it was pure inspiration and nothing else.

Wayside

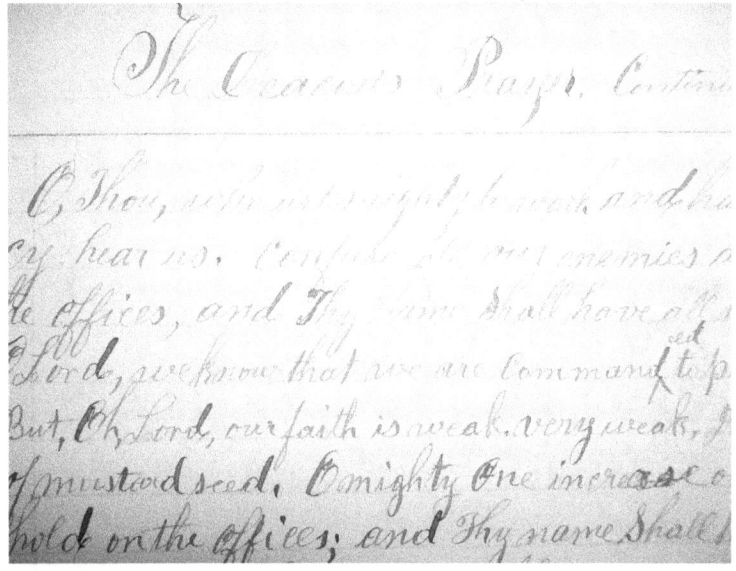

power, just give us the Strength of Sampson
to twist the Lionstail till he yowlps. We need
good of the party and Blaine's sake. O Lord the
ver is running low and we will be bankrupt
the offices. O Lord most mighty help us now,
you back, double, after election. Yea Lord
we will build you a house of Power and Pel
Just give us the offices and you can have o
We are all true Native Americans, and believe
have all the offices i.e. those of the Blaine Stripe
We are against all foreigners especially
but we have to bow to the necessity

us the offices and you can have all
ll true Native Americans, and believ
ffices i.e. those of the Blaine Stripe,
against all foreigners especially th
but we have to bow to the necessity
m all in for Blaines Sake, That
t we need to make the campai
in the name of the machine for
the name and the Machine

CHAPTER TWO

Devotion A Prayer

By

William McFarland

'Wayside'

Greatly to be adored, Lord, God, Almighty, Maker of Heaven and Earth and all that therein is. How can we approach the Invisible. The one from everlasting to everlasting. Still the Unchangeable, Infinite Being, whose word is power, and whose will is law? Heavenly Father, to Thee, we look for help, for love, for light, and understanding. O Thou Invisible One, reveal Thyself in the hearts of the people. Speak to the troubled soul, "Peace be still." There is a want that naught can fill, nothing but thy grace. O for an overflow of Divine Love; love that shall make our souls expand and rejoice in the light of truth. There is a light in the window of God's Free Grace that says to all "Look up and live." We feel to thank Thee that the gates stand "ajar" ready to open to the sincere in heart. There is a beauty, grandeur, and glory in the religion of Jesus Christ that exalts the soul for it reaches from earth to heaven and takes hold on Eternal Life. Yea it fills our hearts with love and makes a heaven below. O Thou Invisible Essence of Light Divine smile upon us, and give us grace for Thou art God, and besides Thee, there is no other, we bow with reverence looking towards thy holy mountain for greater light. Inspire our hearts and voices and fill our souls with the Songs of Salvation. Our hearts begin to warm up as they feel the warm approaches of Thy grace. O! That we may feel it more and more. Yea 'till ever fiber of the soul is quickened into life. Yea more, 'till everyone in this house shall feel and know that God is here. We feel to thank thee more and more, for thy grace is sufficient, and Thy loving kindness, boundless as the seas.

Rejoice O my soul, let everything that hath breath praise the Lord; Praise ye the Lord.

Wayside

O! that we may feel it might... ...ver fibre of the soul is quicken'd ...d every one in this house shall ...od is here. ...O feel to thank The... ...hy Grace is sufficient and Thy ...nd boundless as the seas ...Let every thing that hath ...ord; Praise ye the Lord.

Wayside

CHAPTER THREE

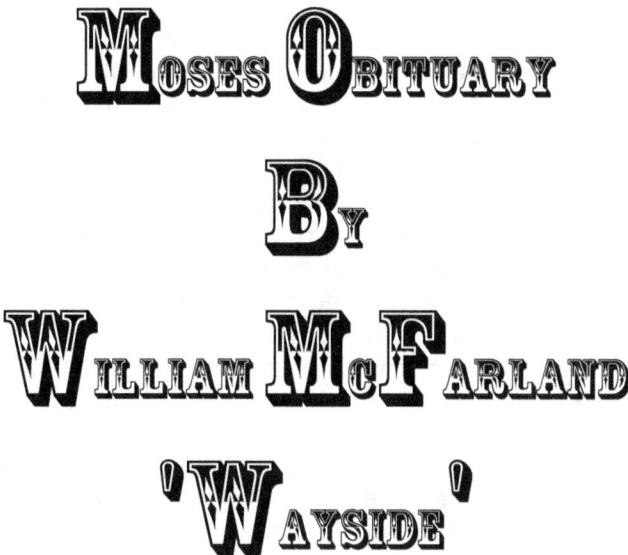

MOSES OBITUARY

BY

WILLIAM McFARLAND

'WAYSIDE'

Died on the top of Mount Pisgah in the land of Moab. - Moses aged one hundred and twenty years. He died three thousand three hundred and thirty-four years ago about the first of August last.

Of the nature of his disease at the time of his death we are not informed with certainty. We presume he died of heart disease as his death was quite sudden and unexpected and there was no doctor called in and no coroner's inquest held over the corpse.

His funeral was different from that of most great men; was unostentatious in character, was quite private and inexpensive; and yet, it must have been sublime and imposing. God, the Great Ruler and mover of World's dug his grave and covered him up so secretly and carefully that no grave robbers could steal the carcass to sell it to the doctors.

Oh, how we would like to have been there hid away privately, and as a witness looked on the solemn scene at the burial. We wonder how the Lord managed to steal this carcass away so secretly and what his friends thought about the matter at the time, and whether they made much search after the remains; whether they employed a detective and put him on the truck while it was fresh.

We would like to know whether the Lord made a hearse out of nothing with horses of fire to carry the body from the top of the mountains of Pisgah, away down into the valley over against Bethpear, there to bury it so secretly that detective orgrave robber has been able to find it "even unto this day!"

Had the account, death and burial of our deceased friend not been written by himself under divine inspiration we could hardly believe the story it seems so remarkable so different from any other great man's burial we ever knew of. Whether God put him into a rose-wood or mahogany casket we, cannot tell, for the reason that there were no fashionable cards or invitations sent out to invite us to the funeral and we are sure there were no newspaper reporters present to write the matter up as a local, a sensational article for some rival paper.

All the note we have of the sad occurrence was written by our deceased friend himself, either before or after the funeral took place, and he being all-fired meek, or the meekest man that ever lived did not like to puff himself at his own burial. We can't help but wander and marvel at the great wisdom, the still and the cunning manifested by the mighty architect of worlds in hiding his dead carcass so secretly.

We have every reason to believe that there was something grand about this old carcass, for we recall that even "Michael" the archangel (whatever that may be) had a row with the Devil about it, "Mike" would have thrashed him soundly if he had not taken back his slander and agreed to do better or something to that effect.

Our deceased friend as we said was a remarkable man in many respects, was the bosom friend, companion and partner of the Great Jehovah, the Creator, ruler and controller of worlds; the one that made the heavens and the earth out of nothing, as well as all contained therein.

Oh, that we had the power to write in full, the account of the doings and sayings of this great man; this man who died so suddenly and was buried so mysteriously. That we might tell how he commenced business by killing a man and ended up his life as a law-giver and a saint. How he met God in a burning bush while he pulled off his shoes and stood in his bare feet on holy ground, we do not know whether he pulled off his breeches at the same time or not; we presume he did, so that God could see his bare legs, that they were shapely and fitted for a holy calling.

We suppose he held his feet out before the fire to keep from taking cold while he conversed with the Lord.

We think he took off his shoes so that the Lord could see that his feet were clean, were fitted to stand on holy ground. As his brother Aaron had bare legs when dressed up, and David appeared in bare legs at a dance before the Lord, we presume this great architect of worlds is never so well pleased as when men wear short breeches; else, why are his priests required as to dress when they come into his immediate presence. As we before said the Lord entered into a partnership with our deceased friend to carry on a grand work; a business that would astound the world; a business that would cause death and disaster, darkness and hailstones, boils and grasshoppers, to terrify and afflict the people comprising a great kingdom or nation. Would cause their water to turn into blood, their land to be covered with frogs and their heads with lice. In this grand compact, his brother Aaron, being a good talker was admitted as a third party to carry on the red tape arrangement.

In this grand compact, God originated and planned, Moses directed, and Aaron executed. All their works, all their sorrows, distress and suffering were to give God a big name among men; to show that he was no slouch; that he understood his business well, better than the best magician in the kingdom; and when he took a fancy towards a people he would do as much, and even more, for them than any other God in the neighborhood.

Although we are taught in this day by our Orthodox friends that "Kings" rule by the grace of God and whosoever resisteth them resisteth the ordinances of God" this rule did not apply in his day. But we suppose there are exceptions to all rules; and in this case, the exception prevailed. In this case, we find God took great pleasure in tormenting a king and while his saving grace was operating on the heart of this king he did not feel that ecstasy and delight that is felt by the modern convert immediately after having his heart changed from nature to grace, at our modern revivals. O the many tricks God with his two trusty partners an old King Pharaoh; the fun they all three had at his expense in spite of his good intentions.

It is said at this day and age of the world that when God works on a man's heart and changes it, he makes it softer, and better, more and more noble and loving.

How different the case with Pharaoh? When God commenced on him he seemed to be a pretty good kind of a fellow with a heart as soft as a woman's but as the work of grace seem to permeate that organ it became harder and harder, until his word was no better, or more reliable than is the word of the drunkard or tobacco chewer and smoker that promises reform.

After playing with him all manner of tricks the trio enticed him and his host into the red sea and drowned them as a rat catcher would do so many rats. We always did admire this God, for his wisdom, his skill and neatness while making for himself such an honorable name; so eminent for justice, so fitting to the great and builder of worlds; and while our mind reverts to Moses, the lawgiver, the overseer for this great ruler, we feel sorry that he died so sudden and so young that his burial was so secret that his bones cannot be found; his sepulcher has never been discovered by the keenest detective; that his resting place is marked by no tombstone; and yet, we owe him much for his history, his laws, his meekness, his skill as a commissary when the larder was empty, as well as his power over nature; all of which acts are known to the theological student, the Doctor of a God who has become feeble and sickly, and who is ministered to by Sixty Thousand priests daily, to keep him alive. All these sayings and doings are grand lessons taught to the pupil by the Sabbath School teacher as bright examples to the Christian upon which he sets his feet as he journeys to his home in the new Jerusalem.

Then farewell Moses, our deceased friend we have heard from you but once since you died on the top of that mountain in the land of Moab, and then you appeared as a materialized spirit at a séance. We hope you and God have a good time together talking over old scenes in which you both were the principal actors! As you gave Pharaoh so much trouble on earth, we hope you will let up on him some in the great hereafter; will give him a little rest and quiet in the heavenly spheres, and if this result be attained, we will close this grand old Obituary. The end.

Wayside

Moses

Died.— On the top of Mount Pisgah in the ___
Moses— aged one hundred and twenty y___
three thousand three hundred and thirty ___
about the first of August last.

Of the nature of his disease at the time of h___
not informed with certainty. We presume ___
disease as his death was quite sudden a___
and there was no doctor called in and ___
quest held over the corpse.

His funeral was different from that of ___

His funeral was different from that of most gre___
was unostentatious in character, was quite p___
inexpensive; and yet it must have been su___
imposing. God, the Great Ruler and Mover of ___
his grave and covered him up so secretly ___
that no grave robbers could steal the carcas___
to the doctors.

Oh, how we would like to have been there hid ___
ratory, and as a witness looked on the solem___
the burial. We wonder how the Lord mana___
this carcass away so secretly and what ___
thought about the matter at the time, and ___
made much search after the remains; ___
___ a detective and put him on ___

Suddenly and was buried so mysteriously that we might tell how he commenced being a man and ended up his life as a lawyer. How he met God in a burning bush and put off his shoes and stood in his bare feet on holy ground. I do not know whether he pulled off his breeches at the time or not; we presume he did, so that God could see that they were shapely and fitted for a holy occasion. I suppose he held his feet out before the fire to keep from getting cold while he conversed with the Lord. We think he took off his shoes so that the Lord could see that his feet were clean, were fitted to stand on. As his brother Aaron had bare legs when and David appeared in bare legs at a dance.

Moses

Lord, we presume this great architect of worlds was pleased as when men wore short breeches; else, as required to keep when they came into his immediate presence when the Lord entered into a partnership used friend to carry on a grand work; a business that toured the world; a business that would cause disaster, darkness and hailstones, boils and grasshoppers and afflict the people comprising a great kingdom and cause their water to turn into blood, their land with frogs and their heads with lice. In this grand scheme being a good father was admitted

...im resisteth the ordinances of God," this rule d...
...pply in his day. But we suppose there are excep...
all rules; and in this case, the exception prevaile...
case, we find God took great pleasure in tormenti...
and while his saving grace was operating on the...
this King he did not feel that ecstasy and delight...
felt by the modern convert immediately after hav...
heart changed from nature to grace. at our mod...
vals. O the many tricks God with his two trusty p...
on Old King Pharaoh; the fun they all track had o...
pense in spite of his good intentions.

It is said at this day and age of the world th...
God works on a man's heart and changes it, he...
it softer, and better, more and more noble an...

Moses

How different the case with Pharaoh? When God com...
he seemed to be a pretty good kind of a fellow with...
a woman's but as the work of grace dam to per...
it become harder and harder, until his word...
more reliable than is the word of the Drunk...
Chewer and Smoker that promises reform.

After playing with him all manner of tricks t...
him and his host into the red sea and drow...
rat catcher would do so many rats. We ador...
this God, for his wisdom, his skill and cuts...
... all such an honorable name;

...or Nature; for his queues and his
...ch acts are known to the theological stu
...a god who has become feeble and sickly,
...red to by sixty thousand priests daily,
...All these sayings and doings are
...t to the pupil by the Sabbath School
...amples to the Christian upon which he
...journeys to his home in the new

...N deceased friend we have heard of from you
...died on the top of that mountain in the land
...appeared as a materialized spirit at a Seance

Jerusalem

Then farewell Moses, I'N deceased
but once since you died in the
Moab, and that you appeared,
We hope you and God have a
Old scenes in which you both
As you gave Pharaoh so mu
will let up on him some in to
a little rest and quiet in the heaven

teacher' as bright examples to the Chr[ist]
sets his feet as he journeys to his
Jerusalem
Then farewell Moses, my deceased friend
but once since you died on the top of th[e]
Moab, and then you appeared as a ma[n]
We hope you and God have a good
Old scenes in which you both were t
As you gave Pharaoh so much troub[le]
will let up on him some in the great
a little rest and quiet in the heavenly sph[ere]

The grand epoch in American histor[y]
announcement of that great princip[le]
right by the old continental Cong[ress]
Thomas Jefferson to, &c. All men
with certain Inalienable rights, l[ib]
erty and the pursuit of happin[ess]
grand legacy of God to man be
the dawn of creation, His fre
eternal as the hills. No man
tate has the moral right to

... gilded the horizon with ... of liberty ... beams. ... Liberty and the rights of man. ... enlisted ... life, for right, for truth and ... were none of weak ... feeble ... at the knee of tyrants ... and kiss the ... to smite them; but men who were ... to dare; men who had staked their ... and offered their lives a willing ... dedication of the sacred trust.

... top of that mountain in the land ... as a materialized spirit at a Seance ... good time together talking over ... were the principal actors! ... trouble on earth, we hope you ... great hereafter; will give him ... spheres, and if this result be ... Obituary   The End

CHAPTER FOUR

SILENCE IN HEAVEN

AND

THE BUTTER-WOMAN

BY

WILLIAM MCFARLAND

'WAYSIDE'

We find it recorded in Holy Writ, that upon a certain occasion there was Silence in Heaven about the space of half an hour. Strange indeed. Passing strange that Heaven should be silent. Can happiness be complete where silence reigns? Or can it be possible that trouble ever comes near Heavens Door? The sweet harp-strings were untouched. The four and twenty elders who continually stand before the throne, crying, "Holy, Holy," stopped suddenly. Doubtful whisperings of one to another were noticed. All Heaven was silent as death; save the inward breathings of the astonished multitude. The commanding general of the Department issued a silent order to all subordinates to hold themselves in readiness to serve at a moment's warning. While light winged Scouts were seen, busily passing to-an-fro and hovering on the out-skirts of Heaven.

The Saints and martyrs who heretofore had made the heavenly dome to ring with their joyful acclamation were dumb, stood trembling with fear, or like scared sheep had fled to some recess impervious situated under the Throne of the Eternal.

The suspense was dreadful and for about half an hour reigned supreme. All roads were barricaded except the Great Highway that lead up to the principal gate; and this was covered by a grand field battery which was already shouted and primed for instant use. Such precaution was unusual and never used only when there is a prospect of something terrible. Only once before had it been chronicled in the records of Heaven that there had been such extreme caution taken, and that was in the days before the world was, when Lucifer the bright son of the morning, conspired against the Highest and brought succession to Heaven and set up a kingdom of his own.

But all things must have an end so must this suspense. At last there appeared in the distance that which caused Heaven itself to feel uneasy and the lesser lights to quake with fear. It was the vision of a women coming alone which the Sentinel on the Watchtower had descried in the distance a woman bearing upon her shoulders two large tubs which appeared to be very heavy which she seemed to be much interested in. She had no escort not even a penny dog but came unannounced and alone.

On arriving near the outskirts of the city she halted and arranged her tubs in order, and then called for the inspector. She said she had taken great pains with this butter and had concluded to bring some of her best to the King as a thank offering for her unbounded prosperity in the world below. This was only the expression of her love and good will toward the Governor.

But, if he did not wish to invest, doubtless there were many who would be very glad to avail themselves of the opportunity. Also she wished to buy a few notions before entering to present to the governor, as a token of her kindness regards for his health and happiness. But no one would buy; neither would they accept of it as a thank-offering. She really did not like the looks of those on the outside so she raised her tubs on her shoulder and moved closer to the gate. It was locked and there was no one outside to give her any assurance; no one but the great gate keeper who watched with jealous eyes her advance to the city.

On arriving at the gates after unloading she knocked at the gate for admission. But not a sound, or a voice greeted her. Feeling somewhat piqued by the delay and disrespect shown by not answering her summons immediately called to the gatekeeper above to open the door and let her come in, for she had eaten and drank in the Lord's vineyard lo! These many years, and besides this she had brought a valuable present in these tubs for the governor, and as she was one of the elect there was no use in parleying about it; so just open the gate and let me move in. But the gate did not open neither did the Sentinel at the gate say a word. The great gatekeeper general who was standing within overheard the words of the woman and peering over the gates said, "Woman, what is it that brings you here? You are certainly out of your latitude. On looking over the books; I find your name recorded in the journal kept for the other side of the house. Now take up your tubs and depart.

After looking wistfully around as if afraid she, heavily depressed in spirit and almost overcome at the sudden change of affairs sorrowfully shouldered her two tubs of butter, and started for the Kingdom of Pluto.

After wandering about, without the city for some time she was suddenly accosted by two individuals clothed in white; who doffing their hat to the lady and bowing politely said "Most noble lady let us show you the way. You are weary and need assistance. We will also help you carry your tubs." The woman felt flattered and thanked them kindly for the proffered help and would gladly accept. The two individuals each taking her by the hand started off in fine spirit down an inclined plain that lead into the Valley of Tophet.

Her two companions guides talked pleasantly of things below and said they were not near so bad as reported.

At last her descent became very rapid being accelerated by her two guides holding her by the hands and running with all their might. She was dreadfully afraid. She would lose her tubs of butter, but she managed to hold on until she reached the outer gate. While she was standing there waiting for her conductors to move on. Her ears were greeted with doleful sounds and dreadful murmurings within. There were yellings and screamings within that made her tremble all over. It seemed as if Pandemonium had broken loose for all Hell was in an uproar.

Suddenly the massive black iron gates rolled back on their hinges revealed a frightful looking object presented himself standing in the gateway and looked more hideous while he scowled on the trembling Butter-Woman, says he to the two guides in mock gravity "Bring her in the master said so" but I guess she won't stay there long, for all Hell is in an uproar over her advent. They are afraid she will try to palm off some of that spurious compound of hers which she calls butter. All Hell is against her, but the Prince of the infernal pit says "Let her come in and bring her tubs with her."

She was brought into a very large hall apparent lighted with gas; but which smelt very much like brimstone. She was very much troubled and could not help it. Things revolved through her mind at a rapid rate. Those Sunday teachings and Sabbath School lessons with the Lake of Fire and Brimstone haunted her continually.

After looking about abstractedly rather in doubt as to her reception being agreeable the Prince (Lucifer) made his appearance in full court dress fantastically arranged which rather dazzled the eyes of our Quon dam -- Butter-Woman. Bowing politely and doffing his hat in true dramatic style; commenced thus, "Most noble Lady of Neponset City! What brought you here? By what strategy did you enter our gates? And who are the ones who brought you here? And what have you in those tubs?

"O most Noble Prince" and Ruler these tubs are both full of Butter. A very choice article made and prepared, expressly prepared for your own table. Only a small remuneration and a resting place in your kingdom do I ask.

I am foot-sore tired travelling to-and-fro, seeking rest, and finding none. Things look strange and everything seems at fault. I have been a lone wanderer on the outskirts of the universe a long time, O, won't you, most noble, Prince will you not shelter and protect a helpless handmaid who has thrown her all at your feet. My greatest desire and efforts shall be in your behalf and to the further prosperity of your Kingdom.

Why did you not stop over at the gates above? I did; but Saint Peter wouldn't let me in, so I was forced to go somewhere else. While rambling around the outskirts of Paradise two ministering spirits both dressed in white came to me, spoke kindly, and offered me their assistance; which I kindly accepted. I did not know who, or, what they were. But they spoke so very pleasant and kind, and being almost tired to death I was constrained to follow. Then you are that great Butter-Woman of Neponset City whose fame has reached to the uttermost part of the earth. It will certainly give me great pleasure to accommodate you. Your case shall be inquired into and if it is possible will make you my "Right-Bower" but all Hell is in an uproar over your advent, and it may cost me my crown if I retain you. The warning words of secession has been run in my ears time and again. Some are in such a terrible rage about that butter of yours they threaten to make fuel of it or dump it into the soap kettle. And besides this the Queen, my wife is so terribly incensed about it your life would be in great danger. You will have to wait in the outer courts for a few days until I can prepare a place for you; and give you a final answer. But don't you offer to sell any butter until the revenue collector comes round. Everything has to be stamped here according to value. Your butter must have the great seal of state after which it may be sold in any part of the Kingdom for its full value.

How long will I have to wait before I can get an answer? "O not long I will hurry up things and report as soon as possible. Where am I to rest while you are gone? Is there any water here? Can I have a drink? My dear Lady I see you are not posted. There are no beds in the outer court and as for water you could not find one drop in the whole kingdom. Everybody here uses liquid sulphur and all prefer it to water. You will soon get used to it.

This was terribly severe on the poor Butter-Woman; for she was hungry, foot sore, and tired all over. But there was no other alternative. His Satanic majesty turned and left her all alone there in the dark to ponder on things uncertain. There the poor disconsolate woman stood waiting oh, how long! The Lord only knows and he won't tell. She had nothing to eat but her nasty, stinking butter and nothing to drink but a pot of liquid sulphur that out-ranked her butter. She could not lay down for there was no bed to rest on. There was no light and everything was dark as pitch. There was no fire nor water, nor anything to comfort or amuse. Nothing to be seen or heard except it be the stifled murmurings of the damned below.

After an age as it seemed had passed when despair had taken fast hold of her she heard a mighty uproar. It seemed as if all Hell's artillery were let loose lightnings and loud thunders flashed and roared hideous sounds mingled with groaning unutterable filled the vast concave and made the building rock from centre to circumference. Our Quon dam Butter-Woman was all the while standing ready to sink.

In the bitterest agony of soul she cries out "What shall I do to be saved!!" At that very moment the door flew open. The King appeared closely followed by a hideous monster whose very nostrils belched forth fire and brimstone. Fly, escape for thy life. There is no place for you here! Take your butter and be gone and be quick about it. "Oh most noble prince do let me have a drink of good pure water for I am awful thirsty."

"No I can't do it. We don't deal in that article
we use nothing but liquid sulpher as a beverage.
Come, hurry yourself and be off for the Queen is a
coming tearing up Heel-Street. She is as mad as she
can be and swears by the infernal pit that she will
make you and your nice butter into soap. She says
her wares need washing and she must have soap to
make things shine. Several high dignitaries of the
church militant will soon be here and we must have
things in readiness to receive them. Come, hurry up,
delays are dangerous. The Queen is coming; get out!"

All trembling with fear she picked up her two
tubs and started for the door. But, Oh! What a sight!
The floor opened! And she saw a cauldron of boiling
hot sulphur waiting to bleach her bones far down
below. The Old Queen made her appearance just as
the woman was trying to retrace her steps and said
"The top of the morning to eye most noble lady, won't
you take a bath? Suiting the actions to the words she
threw the poor woman head foremost into the
burning, boiling liquid below and then threw the tubs
of butter after her. This was the grand finale and
tragic ending of the Great Butter-Woman of Neponset
City. If any one should doubt the correctness of this
story, go to the store, there you will find some of the
soap.

Wayside

Says she to the two guides in mock grav[e]
Master said so,, But I guess she won't stay
Hell is in an uproar over her advent. Th[ey]
try to palm off some of that spurious Con[?]
she calls butter &c &c Hell is against he[r]
the Infernal pit "Says Bring Let her co[me]
tubs with her.

She was brought into a very [?]
lighted with gas; but which smel[l]

[being] agreeable the Prince (Lucifer)
[pla]ce in full court dress fantastically
rather dazzled the eyes of our Quon[dam]
[w]oman, Bowing politely and diff[erent]
Dramatic style; Commenced thus
[of Re]sponse! What brought you her[e?]
did you enter our gates? And
[w]ho brought you here? And wha[t]
tubs,,
[Pr]ince and Ruler These tubs a[re]
[a] very choice article Made and
[pre]pared for your own table. [?]

60

"Why did you not stop over a[t]
I did; but Saint Peter wouldn't [...]
to go somewhere else, While [...]
outskirts of Paradise Two Min[...]
dressed in White came to me, [...]
ed me their assistance; which I [...]
I did not know who, or what [...]
spoke so very pleasant and [...]
most tired to death I was const[...]
Then you are that great Butter [...]

spoke so very pleasant and k[...]
most tired to death I was constrained
Then you are that great Butter-woman
whose fame has reached to the uttermo[st]
It will certainly give me great pleasure
you. Your case shall be inquired; and
I will make you my "Right-Bower," B[...]
an uproar over your advent and i[...]
my crown if I retain you. The warm
secession has been run in my ears tim[...]
Some are in such a terrible rage about [...]
they threaten to make fuel of it or dump[...]
kettle. And besides this the Queen, my [...]
[...] about it your life would be in [...]

my crown if I retain you. The warning [of]
secession has been run in my ears time and [again]
Some are in such a terrible rage about that but
they threaten to make fuel of it or dump it into [a]
kettle. And besides this The Queen, My wife is so
incensed about it your life would be in great d[anger]
You will have to wait in the outer courts for a few d[ays]
I can prepare a place for you; and give you a fin[al]
But don't you offer to sell any butter until the Reven[ue]
comes round. Everything has to be stamped here acc[ording to]
value. Your butter must have the great seal of Sta[te]
which it may be sold in any part of the Kingdom [for its full]
value
How long will I have to wait before I can get an [...]

rible rage about that butter of you[r]
[f]uel of it or dump it into the [troop]
[th]is The Queen, My wife is so terribl[y]
[you]r life would be in great danger.
[. . .] in the outer courts for a few days until
[f]or you; and give you a final answe[r]
[se]ll any butter until the Revenue Collector
[. . .]ing has to be stamped here according to
[m]ust have the great seal of State after
[. . .] in any part of the Kingdom for its ful[l]

comes round. everything has to
value. Your butter must have
which it may be sold in any p
value

How long will I have to wait
" O not long I will hurry up t
possible
Where am I to rest while y
water here? Can I have a d
... you are not p

...rything has to be stamped here according to
...ter must have the great seal of State after
sold in any part of the Kingdom for its full

I have to wait before I can get an answer?
...ll hurry up things and report as soon as

rest while you are gone? Is there any
I have a drink
...ou are not posted. There is no beds in the
...for water you could not find one d...
... Nobody here uses liquid ...

value
"How long will I have to wait before
" O not long I will hurry up things a
possible
"Where am I to rest while you a
water here?" Can I have a drink
"My dear Lady you are not posted.
outer Court and as for water you co
in the whole kingdom, Everybody
and all prefer it to water. You will b

for I am awful thirsty."
"No I cant do it, we dont deal in
nothing but liquid sulpher as
hurry yourself and be off for
tearing up Heel street she is
and swears by the infernal pit t
and your nice butter into soo
washing and she must soap t
high dignitaries of the church
we must have things in rea

Silence in Heaven

Come, hurry up, delays are dangero[us]
coming; Get out!

All trembling with fear she pi[cked]
tubs and started for the door. But,
The floor opened! and she saw a ca[uldron]
sulpheir waiting to bleach her bone[s]
The Old Queen made her appearan[ce]
was trying to retrace her steps an[d]
morning to use Most noble lady, [

delays are dangerous, The Queen i[s]
[] with fear she picked up her two
[] the door. But, Oh! what a sight!
[] she saw a cauldron of boiling hot
bleach her bones far down below.
[] her appearance just as the woman
her steps and said "The top of the
[n]oble lady, won't you take a bath?
[] words she threw the poor woman
[] Burning boiling Liquid belo[w]

CHAPTER FIVE

LOVE OF MONEY

BY

WILLIAM McFARLAND

'WAYSIDE'

What is gambling? The evil genius of the human race. A festering sore on the body politic. A wolf in sheep's clothing. Its very presence produces contamination and breaks out in eruptions of evil only.

The love of money is said to be the root of all evil, and well do our money-crates know how, and do use this power. They know, when, where, and how to strike, when they wish to carry a point. Our late corporation election was no exception to the rule. I really pity the poor tool, who sold his honor and good conscience for a mess of porridge. Two wrongs never make a right, and these individuals who use this power will soon learn that chickens come home to roast, and that crime of bribery, like murder will out. When professed Christian men can smile at corruption, and roll it under their tongues like a sweet morsel, we may well tremble for the liberties of our beloved country. This intimidation business is a twin brother to bribery, and should be denounced by all honest people.

CHAPTER SIX

EARLY RISING

BY

WILLIAM MCFARLAND

'WAYSIDE'

Some people have very queer notions about getting up early. Some think it gives them a good appetite and red cheeks. Some think the early bird catches the worm. But I am like the baby, just give me a plenty of sleep, and I will grow, and get fat, and when I get my nap out, I won't be cross and ugly.

How much better it is to wake up with a smile on your face than a frown. All young people require a good deal of sleep. They should go to bed early, so as to get their nap out. Nothing is so injurious to health, as to rob youth of its required rest. A sweet, deep sleep and undisturbed rest, is best for soul and body. The girls and boys romp and play, until tired nature asks repose.

Then play while the sun shines. But when night comes on seek that comfortable little bed that me has made for you. Tho cozy little cot so snug, so neat and clean. Then close your eyes in blissful sleep, and dream, per chance you'll dream of Mary.

To dream of one you love so well, will do you good. Those den smiles of Dream Land, that make the heart to flutter with delight, are sweet indeed.

In dreams I often see the old home. The place of my early childhood. Its mountains, its hills and valleys greens, still remain the same. I see the village lawn and commons those selfs ones who used to meet me there. In dreams, I see the old cabin - school house on the hill and all the boys and who used to play with me. O, what rapturous delight fills my heart as I fancied grasped the hands of Mary and Jane. Their blushing cheeks and bright sparkling eyes all a glow with that sweet and tender expression of love and delight which always abound in your innocent hearts.

Then disturb not the sleeping child, but let it sleep and dream 'till sunrise. Then fresh and blooming and tening, clear and bright, those youthful will open body and soul all refreshed, and vigorous; within the heart, light in the eyes and love in the soul, both soul and body. all refresh will delight to meet the rising god of day. O bright winged Goddess of Love smile on the sleeping beauties. Let nought disturb their resting place, or, mar their sleeping hours. Gather all the little ones who are weary and tired, under the still quiet folds of thy soft, sweet, tender, and loving embrace. Shield and protect them in that sweet reverie; and shed a Halo of Glory over the sleeping child.

1.

O let me sail the balmy deep,
And gather rest in sweetest sleep;
'Til scented Zephyrs ope mine eyes;
'Til golden beauty gilds sunrise.

2.

Then fresh, and blooming, bright and gay,
We'll rise to meet the god of day;
With buoyant hearts in this glad hour,
Greet nature in her blooming bower.

3.

When dewdrops glisten in the trees
When fragrant odors fill the breeze,
When birds first sing in morning skies,
Mine eyes will open at sunrise.

4.

When tired nature calls for rest,
When trouble, toil distract the breast,
When lengthen'd shadows onward creep,
Then comes the sweet refreshing sleep.

5.

Let nought disturb the sleeper 'till,
The morning song of Jack and Jill;
'Til wakes the bird in leafy bower,
To greet with song the morning hour.

6.

As toiling millions onward sweep,
Forgetful of the hours of sleep;
The sweetest boon to mortals given,
The rest that makes our earth a Heaven.

7.

My dear kind friend don't be a pest,
But let the little sleeper rest;
'Til golden hues gild sunny skies,
'Til laughing birds greet bright sunrise.

8.

When crows the cock at early morn;
When sharp and shrill he sounds his horn;
Then soon we hear that dreadful noise,
"Come, hurry up, you girls and boys."

9.

Come, hurry up, come right away;
You know we have to wash today.
O, dear, 'Says Ma" you sleepy head!
'Tis hard to get you out of bed!

10.

I rolled me over in my bed;
I rubb'd my eyes and scratched my head.
O, what means all this Hurly Burly?
This everlasting "Get up early."

11.

What makes my head to swim around,
When out of bed I sometimes bound?
What makes me stretch, and yawn, and swagger?
And often like a drunk man stagger?

12.

Sometimes we stay out late at night,
Then Pa says "Girls this is not right;
We go to bed, feel somewhat surly;
Well knowing Ma will call us early.

13.

Sometimes we have to jump up quick;
For Pa is coming with a stick,
To lick the ones he loves so dearly;
And learn them all to get up early.

14.

You know it sometimes feels so good;
To be in a delightful mood,
Of sweetest sleep while night rolls on,
A dreaming of a darling one.

15.

Now all mankind is in such strife,
Which causes me to say, "What is life?"
And what makes all this "Hurly Burly"?
This everlasting "Get up early?"

16.

While resting in sweet slumbers bower,
O, let me sleep the morning hour;
And dream of love and paradise,
'Til birds shall warble out sunrise.

17.

Then all refresh'd, and bright and gay,
We'll sing with birds the morning lay;
A pleasant theme no "Hurly Burly."
But soft and sweet yes this is early.

18.

Now girls and boys I love you dearly;
And my advice is get up early;
Then go to bed before 'tis mine,
You'll then be sure to wake up fine.

19.

The sluggard saunters round til 'leven,
And then he sleeps 'till after seven;
But if he wakes cries "Hurly Burly"
You always wake me up too early.

Wayside

Early Rising

Then play where the sunshines.
Seek that comfortable little bed that
cozy little cot so snug, so neat and cl
in slipful sleep, and beanm; perchan
To dream of one you love so well, a
tens miles of Dream Land that me
delight, are sweet indeed.
In dreams I often see the home. The
It mountains, its hills and valley
same. Tree on the village lawn a
to meet me there.

CHAPTER SEVEN

TEMPERANCE

BY

WILLIAM MCFARLAND

'WAYSIDE'

At a great wedding in Cana of Galilee when Christ and some of his disciples were present some of the guests got so very much accelerated they couldn't tell colored water from wine. When the Prodigal Son returned to his father's house they made a feast, and killed the fatted calf. And I guess the good old father tapped the barrel. There was music and dancing; all had become merry over the influence of wine. The prodigal's brother who happened to be a crank and a bigot besides reproved his father for indulging in such festivities and becoming so merry over the profligate sons return saying "I have been with you lo! These many years I have been a good son, never was drunk in my life drink nothing but pure cold-water. Yet you never killed a fatted calf nor made a feast like this for me."

It is written in the Holy Scriptures that wine maketh glad the heart of man, but, that milk will do for babes. Now the Bible is chock full of wine and strong drink from Genesis to Revelations. And any man who pretends to the truth as revealed in the Bible cannot be a prohibitionist.

The Holy Bible is a book of infinite variety and boundless sublimity, which is the strongest proof of its divine origin. Good and evil are laid out into equally endless proportions, which is for the instruction and benefit of mankind. It is this universal variety and difference of opinion that brings us into prominence. St. Paul said "Where iniquity abounds grace doth much more abound. Transgression is the school of experience. It is the main spring of all our happiness. It is that which brings truth to light. If it was not for the blunders and errors which we commit in this world, the very light of truth would fade from sight. Good and evil is God's work, which is placed herein equally endless proportions and varieties; on which all mankind everywhere is to feel, live and learn.

This very school of experience helps to qualify us for all stations in life, and in the world to come.

Without forgiveness there can be no happiness, and without transgression there can be no forgiveness. Talk about man enjoying happiness with knowing the difference between good and evil is the merest twaddle. It is a man stuffing himself when he is not hungry. There is no logic nor good sense in such philosophy. Any man who deals in such trash as a beverage; don't know what he is talking about and should be fed on milk 'till his beard grows.

The great diversity of mind, matter, and opion which is everywhere present in the human organism is proof of positive of God's omnipotent work.

Good and evil combined is God's work for it makes a perfect whole. They are a product of a master mind in making up the sum total of all happiness. None but a God of infinite might and mind could produce such a medley; such a wonderful combination of endless variations, all working for harmony without a jar, or screw loose.

Wayside

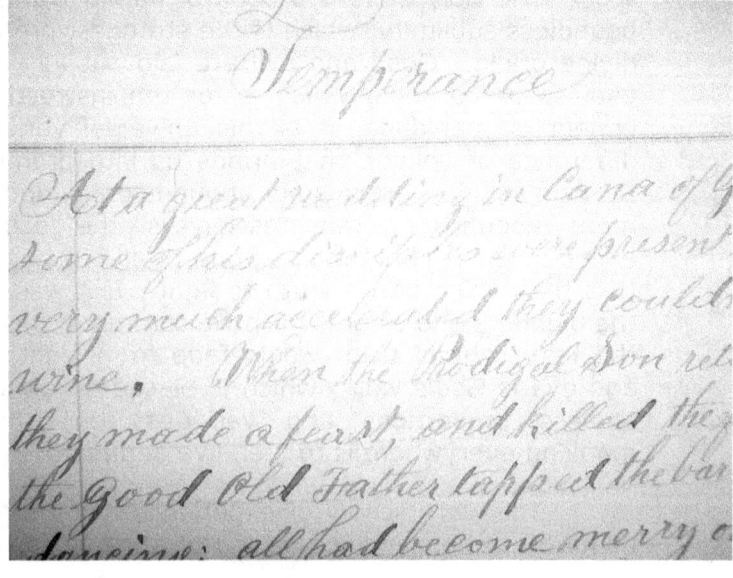

... proportions, which is for the instruct...
...of mankind. It is this universal vari...
...ence of Opinion that brings us into pro...
...St Paul said "where iniquity abounds...
...more abound. Transgression is th... scho...
...It is the mainspring of all our happine...
...which brings truth to light. If it was...
...ders and errors which we commit in th...
...very light of truth would fade from...
...Good and Evil is Gods work, which is...
...equally endless proportions and vari...
...It mankind everywhere is to feed, live an...

This very school of experience...
all stations in life, and in the wa...
Without forgive... there can be no...
gression there can be no forgiveness...
piness with knowing the difference...
merest twaddle. It is a man stuffing...
There is no logic nor good sense in...
who deals in such trash as a b...
...and
...should be but...

present in the human organism is
nipotent work.
Good and evil combined is Gods no
whole. They are a product of a master
Sum total of all happings. No
and mind could produce such a
ful combination of endless variet
many without a jar, or screw loo

s, which is for the instruction
It is this universal variety a
on that brings us into promin
"Where iniquity abounds gra
. Transgression school of
pring of all our happiness.
truth to light. If it was not
which we commit in this
truth would fade from sigh

...s this universal variety and differ...
...that brings us into prominence.
...here iniquity abounds grace doth much...
...ransgression is the school of experience.
...ng of all our happiness. It is that...
...th to light. If it was not for the blun-
...hich we commit in this world; the...
...th would fade from sight
...God's work, which is placed herein...
...s proportions and varieties; on which...
...her is to feed, live and learn

...anism is proof positive of God's Om...

...s God's work for it makes a perfect...
...of a master mind in making up the...
...s. None but a god of infinite might...
...such a medley; such a wonder-...
...s variations, all working in her...
...screw loose.

Wayside

CHAPTER EIGHT

What Is Christianity?

By

William McFarland

'Wayside'

What is Christianity? And what is the religion of the Bible? It used to be taught when I was a boy, that the religion of Jesus Christ was above every earthly consideration; that its value could neither be weighed nor measured. But this is a progressive age and things have greatly changed. Temperance takes the lead now. No church can have a good congregation except on Temperance night, Why is this? Is prohibition of greater value or superior to Christianity? Or has the old version played out? We know that one of our most eminent divines said that "Christianity was not quite sufficient to make a good radical temperance man." A visit to any of our churches on temperance night reveals this; that infidels unbelievers and even atheists are permitted to teach in the family of the faithful. Even scoffers of religion are given a high seat in front on temperance night. But it is an age of progress and mankind is learning very fast. Christianity and the Bible have had a terrible set back by this new fangled doge of Prohibition miss called temperance. I believe in temperance and intend to live and die a temperance man, but if prohibition is better than the religion of Jesus Christ and his apostles I fail to see it. But it may be that I am blind in my own conceit and can't see clearly.

What is Christianity?
What is Christianity? And what is the
It used to be taught when I was a boy, the
Christ was above every earthly consideratio
neither be weighed nor measured. But thi
things have greatly changed. Temperance tak
Church can have a good congregation exe
Why is this? Is prohibition of greater va
tianity? Or has the old version played
f our most eminent Divines said that "Chris
sufficient to make a good radical tempera

And what is the religion of the Bible?
en I was a boy, that the religion of Jesus
arthly consideration; that its value could
asured. But this is a progressive age and
. Temperance takes the lead now. No
congregation except in temperance night,
ttion of greater value or superior to Chris-
version played out? We know that one
said that "Christianity was not quite
radical temperance man." A writ

of our most eminent Divines said that "Christianity was
sufficient to make a good radical temperance man" in
to any of our churches on temperance might reveals this f
Deists, unbelievers and even Atheists are permitted
the family of the faithful, even scoffers of religion are give
on temperance and in front. But in age of progress and mankind is
very fast. Christianity and the Bible have had a ter
by this new fangled dogs of Prohibition miscalled te
I believe in temperance and intend to live and die
man, but if prohibition is better than the religion of Je
and his apostles I fail to see it. But it may be that
in my own conceit and cant see clearly

The Bible Better

The Devil had a great spite against Job, and the way the Dev
conspired with the Most High, and terribly afflicte

temperance might reveals this fact, that
even Atheists are permitted to teach i
en Scoffers of religion are given a high
age of progress and mankind is learning
and the Bible have had a terrible set bac
e of Prohibition miscalled temperance
and intend to live and die a temperan
better than the religion of Jesus Christ
see it. But it may be that I am blind
l Cant see Clearly

CHAPTER NINE

THE TILE SETTER

BY

WILLIAM McFARLAND

'WAYSIDE'

The Devil had a great spite against Job, and the way the story reads, conspired with the "Most High" and terribly afflicted him. They robbed him of all his possessions, burned his houses with fire and took all his children into captivity, besides all this dreadful calamity they sorely afflicted him with boils not even leaving a big enough well place to sit on. Yet Job bore up man fully and never repined once against Providence. But if that is the way to make a good man better, I don't hanker after it.

n my own conceit and cant see clearly

The Title Settler

The Devil had a great spite against Job, and the way
Conspired with the most High, and terribly
They robbed him of all his possessions burned his
and took all his children into captivity, be
but calamity they sorely afflicted him with
big enough well place to sit on. Yet Job bore
never repined once against Providence
way to make a good man better. I don't ha

---

mperance and [...]
[pro]hibition is better than the religion of Jesus Christ
is I fail to see it. But it may be that I am blind
[conce]it and cant see clearly

The Title Settler

[g]reat spite against Job, and the way the story reads,
th most High, and terribly afflicted him
in of all his possessions burned his houses with fire
[h]is children into captivity, besides all this dreadf[ul]
they sorely afflicted him with boils not even hav[ing]
[w]ell place to sit on. Yet Job bore up manfully a[nd]
once against Providence. But if that is the
a good man better, I don't hanker after it.

CHAPTER TEN

GENTLY FALLS THE

BEAUTIFUL SNOW

BY

WILLIAM McFARLAND

'WAYSIDE'

Gently falls the beautiful snow, floating noiselessly down from the upper deep, to cover us with a mantle of charity, the cold, brown earth with a mantle and hide with its crystal covering the sleeping flowers. While watching the snowflakes fall, thoughts of former days come up too thick for utterance. In fancy I re-visit my old native home in that beautiful valley (the Shenandoah) bounded by the ridge for ever blue, whose tall peaks kiss the clouds as the stoop to rest on its snowy summit; and the tall waving pines bow their ever-green heads in lofty grandeur to the passing breeze.

Many years have fled since last I saw my old sunny home and its beautiful ridge of blue. But can a man forget his native state; the home of his early childhood, where he first learned to lisp those sweetest words "My Mother."

"O give me back my native hills,

Rough, rugged, though, they be;

No other clime, no other hills

Are half so dear to me."

But time still rolls on and I a wanderer here. Already the frosts of many winters tinges my temples with its silver grey. While deep furrows of care and time circle the brow tells the tale, "Old Age" "Wayside" is swiftly traveling down the steep decline to hide himself with the sleeping flowers.

Magazine Letters

Gently falls the Beautiful Snow

...the beautiful snow, floating noiselessly down from...
...antle of charity, the cold brown earth ... with a...
...vering the sleeping flowers. While watchi...
...mer days come up too thick for utterance. ...
...that beautiful valley (the Shenandoah) be...

Gently falls the beautiful snow, floating n...
...as with a mantle of charity, the cold bro...
its crystal covering the sleeping flowe...
thoughts of former days come up too thick...
native home in that beautiful valley (the...
for ever Blue, whose tall peaks kiss...
snowy summits, and ^those the tall waving pi...
grandeur to the passing breeze.
Many years have fled since last I gaze...

CHAPTER ELEVEN

PRAYER FOR THE STRICKEN SOUTH

BY

WILLIAM MCFARLAND

'WAYSIDE'

DATED 1878

O, Lord, God, Almighty; we have sinned against Heaven and in Thy Sight. Our transgressions have multiplied until they reach the very Gates of Heaven. We have trampled on the mercies of God until the very rocks cry out against us. We have indulged in that which was an abomination. Our sins have grown the mountains high. Our steps take hold on Hell. In an evil hour, when men began to say "There is no God," flushed with the success of their own sinful indulgences; covered and bathed in the blood, of their fellow mortals; thy pent up wrath burst forth in all its fury. And now the wailings of those poor deluded and stricken mortals are heard throughout the land.

The great ones of the earth tremble at the majesty of thy power, and cry "Lord save us." Thy name has became magnified. Thou hast made them to call on Thee. Hear us O, God, in Heaven thy lofty habitation; and give ear to our supplication, because Thou are God and besides Thee, there is no other.

We have sinned greatly. But is not Thy grace sufficient? Has our light gone out forever? Is there no salvation for Thy stricken people? O, Lord, God Almighty help us. Thine arm alone can save. There is no hope, no ray of light, for all is dark. The suffering, the dying, and the dead, cover the land. O, God break the spell of this destroying power. Let the light of Thy countenance smile on and save this afflicted people. Call away the Destroying Angel; and may this visitation of Thy Providence be burned into a blessing. That all may know that Thou art God. That in Thy hands are life and death. That Thou art a God whose word is power and whose will is law.

Remove this pestilence and give us rest. Pour on the oil wine and give us the Balm of Consolation. Let Thy righteousness be exalted among the people, and Thy name be glorified. For Thou alone art excellent. Thy exalted goodness stands supreme. Thy loving-kindness is as boundless as the sea. Thou art High, Ever-all, Blessed for Evermore.

Wayside

Prayer for the Stricken South.

O, Lord, God, Almighty; we have sinned ag[ainst]
Heaven and in Thy sight. Our transgressions have r[isen]
until they reach the very Gates of Heaven. We h[ave]
on the mercies of God until the very rocks cry out a[gainst us]
We have indulged in that which was an abomini[on]
Sins have grown like Mountains high. Our Steps
on Hell. In an evil hour, when men began t[o say there]
is no God, flushed with the success of their own s[elf indul]
gences; Covered and bathed in the blood of their fel[low man]
Thy pent up wrath burst forth in all its fury. A[nd]
wailings of those poor deluded and stricken morta[ls]
throughout the land.

The Great ones of the Earth tremble at the m[anifestations of thy]
power, and Cry "Lord save us", Thy name
magnified. Thou hast made them to call on
God, in Heaven thy lofty habitation; a[nd hear]
our supplication, because Thou art God
[T]hee, there is no other.

Prayer for the Stricken South

We have sinned greatly. But is not Thy Grace sufficien[t]
our light gone out forever? Is there no salvation for Thy [?]
people? O Lord, God Almighty help us. Thine [?] a[?]
save. There is no hope, no ray of light, for all [?]ark. The
the dying, and the dead, cover the land. O, God brea[k]
spell of this destroying power. Let the light of Thy coun[t]
smile on and save this afflicted people. Call away [?]
[?]roying Angel; and may this visitation of Thy Prov[?]
turned into a blessing. That all may know that I[?]
That in Thy hands are life and death. That Thou [?]
whose word is power and whose will is law.
Remove this pestilence and give us rest. Pour [?]
vine and give us the Balm of Consolation. Le[?]
[?]usness be exalted among the people, and Th[y]
Glorified. For Thou alone art excellent. Th[y]
[?]oodness stands supreme. Thy Loving k[?]
[?]oundless as the Sea. Thou art High, Ever [?]
[f]or Evermore.

Prayer for the Stricken South.

O, Lord, God, Almighty; we have sinne[d]
[Hea]ven and in Thy sight. Our trangressions ha[ve]
[un]til they reach the very Gates of Heaven. [W]
the mercies of God until the very rocks cry o[ut]
have indulged in that which was an abom[ination]
[our sin]s have grown like Mountains high. Our st[eps]
[to] Hell. In an evil hour, when men bega[n]
[to ig]nore God, flushed with the success of their own
[for]ces; Covered and bathed in the blood of their f[oes]

Prayer for the Stricken South

We have sinned greatly. But is [our]
our Light gone out forever? Is there [hope for our]
people? O Lord, God Almighty hea[r us,]
save. There is no hope, no ray of li[ght]
the dying, and the dead, cover the
spell of this destroying power. Let

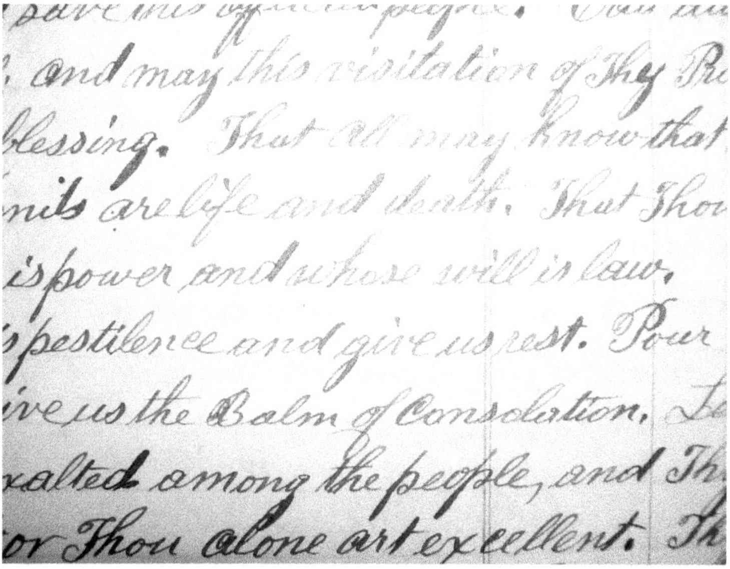

save this afflicted people. Thou a
and may this visitation of Thy Pr
blessing. That all may know that
nits are life and death. That Thou
is power and whose will is law.
pestilence and give us rest. Pour
ive us the Balm of Consolation. Le
xalted among the people, and Th
or Thou alone art excellent. Th

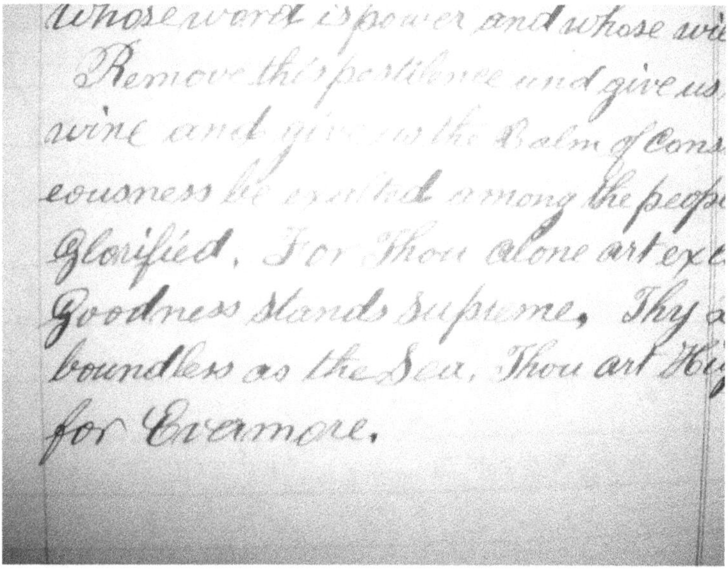

whose word is power and whose wi
Remove this pestilence and give us
wine and give us the Balm of Cons
eousness be exalted among the peop
Glorified. For Thou alone art exc
Goodness stands supreme. Thy
boundless as the Sea. Thou art Hi
for Evermore.

...this afflicted people. Call away the De-
...may this visitation of Thy Providence be
...g. That all may know that Thou art God.
...re life and death. That Thou art a God
...ver and whose will is law.
...ence and give us rest. Pour on the Oil
...the Balm of Consolation. Let Thy Right—
...d among the people, and Thy name be
...ou alone art excellent. Thy exalted
...upreme. Thy Loving-kindness is as

...d give us the Balm of Consolation
...be exalted among the people, and
..., For Thou alone art excellent.
...s stands supreme. Thy Loving
... as the Sea. Thou art High, Ev
...amore.

is power and whose will is law.
pestilence and give us rest. Pour on the Oil
ive us the Balm of Consolation. Let Thy Right—
xalted among the people, and Thy name be
or Thou alone art excellent. Thy exalted
nds supreme. Thy Loving-kindness is as
the Sea, Thou art High, Over all, Blessed
re.

Wayside

CHAPTER TWELVE

AMERICA

By

WILLIAM MCFARLAND

'WAYSIDE'

My country, my home, and my native land. Her verdant plains and templed hills rise in majestic grandeur before me.   The long line of countless numbers that come swarming to our shores proclaim to the world that this is the Eldorado; the land of liberty. Who can measure the length, breadth, height and depth of that word "Liberty?" None but the brave and free. Here we behold the grand array of intellect in full regalia marching on to greatness.   This is positive proof that knowledge is power; and, that man is the architect of his own fortune.

"Home, Sweet Home, is the happy consummation of that which brings peace, joy, and comfort to all of the sons and daughters of America. "My Native Land, Home of the Free!"

Whose great inland seas and mighty rivers swarm with the products of life and the commerce of her own industry.

A climate suited to all tastes or desires and filled with every luxury that heart or soul could ask. A land whose very name makes sweet the melodies of liberty. Yea more. A land where the sun's brightest rays reflect the grandeur, glory, and perfection of the beauties of nature which adore the mansions of the free.   This is my country, my home and my native land. It is the place where freedom reigns.

We see the bright Bow of Promise which circles above and crowns the hills with a halo of glory. It stands as a witness between God and man as a surety of his goodwill that endures forever. We feel and know that God is here, because it is the Land of the Free and the Home of the Brave and true Patriots all each other greet and hail with joy unbounded, the swelling songs of Freedom, God and my Native Land.

Land where my father died!

Land of the Pilgrim's pride!

From every mountain side!

Let freedom ring!

My country, my home, and my own Native Land.

In the beginning God said "Let there be light" and there was light. This is the light of love that illumines the understanding and sets the soul a blaze.

The heroic signers of that immortal Declaration on the Fourth of July 1776 breathed the spirit of that light. That light was the love of liberty and the light of home for it places a window in Heaven and says to all "Look up and live." It is that light which marks the trump of progress which is kindled in every breast and makes us men. This light had taken deep root in the great American heart previous to the Revolution. And when those immortal words were announced to the world; it was a Divinity that marked their utterance.

When Freedom from her mountain height,

Unfurled her standard in the air;

She decked the azure robes of night,

And set the stars of glory there.

The grand epoch in American history was the announcement of those great principles of eternal right by the Old Continental Congress through Thomas Jefferson viz "All men are endowed with certain unalienable rights, to wit, life liberty and the pursuit of happiness. This is the grand legacy of God to man bequeathed from the dawn of creation. It is God's law and eternal as the hills. No man, King nor Potentate has the moral right to set aside these privileges which are God given, nor, abridge to the rights of any in the enjoyment of these elements for they are the common property of all and belong to all. We as an independent, free people hold to these rights which are as sacred to us as the sun that shines, the rain that falls or the air we breathe. It is God's gift man; which remains forever eternal as the hills. It was for the perseverance of this great principle that engaged our forefathers in that mighty struggle for life, liberty, and independence.

The Star of Hope gilded the horizon with festoons of liberty waving in the sun-beams. All hearts were fired with a holy zeal to strike for Liberty and the rights of man. The great lights of that day enlisted for life, for light, for truth and for justice. They were none of weak-kneed, nor, feeble minded who bow at the knee of tyrants and kiss the hand that is raised to smite them; but men who were willing to do, and to dare; men who had staked their all on their country's cause, and offered their loves a willing sacrifice in vindication of the sacred trust. Jefferson, Adams, Hancock, Henry, Payne and all the signers of that Immortal Declaration standing with heads uncovered in the presence of Heaven with the sunlight of truth beaming from their countenances said We, as a right, out to be, and shall be free. God is with us, truth is on our side, then who can stand against us.

Heaven smiled when they signed the grand old parchment. The Goddess of Liberty hovered over the continental army and shed tears of grace over a struggling people contending for the rights of man.

After a terrible struggle for seven long years in doubt and uncertainty, with a seemingly all powerful foe, victory perched herself on the Standard of Liberty. Then such a shout went up astonished the world, "Glory to God in the highest, peace on earth, and good will to men" came sounding from every tongue and echoed from every hill. Brave men wept for joy. We had gained the Pearl of greatest price. That which places man in the highest scale of intellectual existence, i.e. midway from nothing to the Deity.

We had vindicated our faith on the field of battle. Our success was the triumph of Liberty over Despotism. It was written in the blood of our martyred citizens and proven to the world that liberty was the dearest treasure that ever was given to man. And that God the great source of life, light, and love was on our side. Though, truth crushed and bleeding, would rise and rule, sovereign in the ascendant.

All civilized nations of the globe stood in abject wonder and astonishment at the grandeur and glory of our achievements. The love of liberty had kindled a blaze that could not be smothered. That great principle of self-government "The right of life, liberty, and the pursuit of happiness" had taken deep root, and began to swell and move and surge among the people of the old world. They felt, and heard, and saw the triumphs of liberty in the new.

They saw that little band of patriots who had staked their all on their country's cause, were now rejoicing with joy unspeakable in the broad, bright sunlight of liberty. The beacon fires of Free-men and Free-women were kindled on every hill and blazing from every hearth stone.

The swarming millions of the Old World saw the light and felt the fires of liberty kindling in their own breasts set sail for the New World.

Rejoice, O my soul! Let every-thing that hath breath join in the general jubilee. Yea! Blaze on thou glorious light until all nations, peoples and tongues shall come to a full knowledge of the rights of man and joy and rejoice in the universal sunlight of freedom. The Tree of Liberty has taken deep root in the great American heart. Under its wide spreading branches repose all of her sons and daughters. Millions beyond the big water look with longing hearts beating with intense emotion and with outstretched arms to the Land of Liberty.

The monuments of Freedom stand recorded in the temple of justice, whose spires reach to the very heavens and the pillars of divine glory descend from above and rest forever on its summit.

This land is a home for the distressed and persecuted of all nations. At this day and age of progress, the best blood and the most intelligent of the Old World come swarming to our shores.

This is a Heaven-favored land, because it is the home free. A land of unsurpassed fertility; whose broad plains and almost boundless prairies teem with the richest blessings of life to man. A land of free speech, free press, free schools, and an independent free people. A land where superstition, bigotry, and religious intolerance have to take a back seat. The freedom of thought, the freedom of soul. The home of the brave and free.

The inquisition, the thumb-screw, the frying pan and guillotine were once the ruling power; but now they are only known in history and numbered among the things that were. They are only remembered for their brutality, for the ignorance of the ages and the absence of liberty.

It was a despotism produced by tyrants; liberty was crushed, reason failed, and the voice of suffering humanity appealed in vain. But the Star of Hope arise in the west. At first it was not larger than a man's hand; but soon it spread and the light was seen from far. Now its light is seen in every corner of the earth.

I see it in this vast multitude. I see it in this mighty sea of upturned faces. I see it in the light of liberty beaming from every countenance. That which I see before me today is proof that God is love, and that the right to life, liberty and the pursuit of happiness is the inherent right of all mankind.

I see it in your happy faces. I see it in your laughing eyes. I see it in this mighty crowd. I hear its echo in the boom cannon and in the rolling drum. I hear it in the multitude of little voices that have come to swell the general joy by chiming in on the grand chorus of liberty, union, and the rights of man.

This is my country. It is your country. It is our country. It is the Land of the Free; and home of the brave. Shine on thou great and glorious land of Liberty, until the whole world shall be filled with the light of thy countenance.

Columbia, the Birth-right of Freedom was bought with the blood of our fathers. The mighty conflict opened up at Bunker-Hill and closed at Yorktown. The God of Battles and a Washington to lead us gave us victory, peace and happiness and now over fifty millions of people can rejoice together in the sunlight of liberty.

This great National Day; the day of Freedoms new birth is hailed with delight by every true American heart. The watch fires of liberty are blazing from every hill, valley, and plain from the Atlantic to the Pacific, and the songs of freedoms triumph are swelling up in tumultuous joy all over the land on this our glorious Independence Day.

Wayside

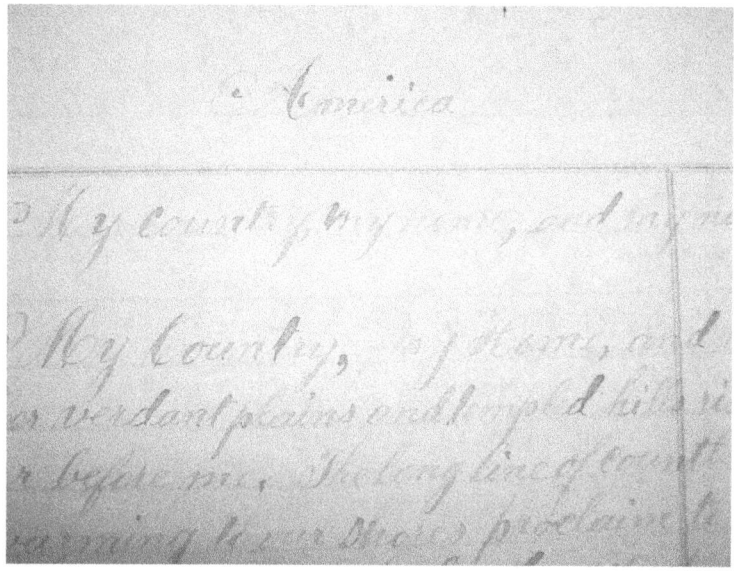

... My Native Land. Home of the brave ...
seas and mighty ... wh...
seas and mighty rivers swarm wit...
of life and the commerce of her own
A climate suited suited to all tastes o...
filled with every luxury that heart o...
A land whose very name makes
odies of Liberty. Yea More. A land
brightest rays reflect the grandeur g...
fection of the beauties of nature whe...
mansions of the free. This is my co...

... Whose great inter...
y rivers swarm with the produ...
n merce her own industry.
d suited to all tastes or desires a...
luxury that heart or soul could a...
very name makes sweet the w...
Yea More. A land where the ...
flect the grandeur glory, and p...
ities of nature which adorn t...
... This is my country, my ...

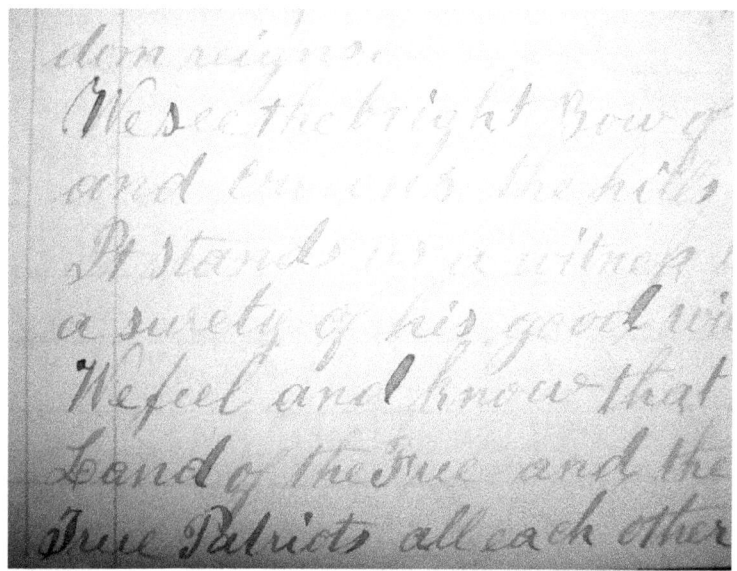

with joy unbounded, the swelling songs
my Native Land

Land where my Father
Land of the Pilgrims p
From every mountain s
Let Free tom ring!!

and my own Native Land.
In the beginning God said "L th

The grand epoch in American histor...
...nouncement of those great inalienable
right by the Old Continental Cong...
Thomas Jefferson say... All men
with certain Inalienable rights, ...
...erty and the pursuit of happiness...
...grand legacy of God to man...
the crown of creation. It is god...
...eternal as the hills. No man...
...tate has the moral right to set aside...

America

...which are God given, nor abridge t...
...enjoyment of these elements for they are
all and belong to all. We as a kind...
to these rights which are as sacred...
...shines, the rain that falls and the...
God's gift to man, which remains fore...
...for the preservation faithful pres...

CHAPTER THIRTEEN

ORATION 4TH OF JULY

BY

WILLIAM McFARLAND

"WAYSIDE"

My country, my home, and my native land. Her verdant plains and templed hills rise in majestic grandeur before me. The long line of countless millions that come swarming to our shores proclaim her the Eldorado of the world, the land of liberty. Who can measure the length, breadth, and depth of that word "Liberty"? None but the brave and free. 'Tis here we behold the grand array of intellect in full regalia, marching on to greatness. This is proof positive that knowledge is power; and, that man is the architect of his own fortune. "Home sweet Home" is the happy consummation of liberty that which brings peace, joy, and comfort to all of the sons and daughters of liberty (America).

"My Native Land" her great inland-seas, and mighty rivers swarm with the products of life and the commerce of her own industry. A climate suited to all tastes and desires, and filled with every luxury. A land whose very name makes sweet the melodies of liberty yea more. A land where the sun's brightest rays reflect the grandeur, glory, and perfection of the beauties of nature which adorns the mansions of the free; i.e. the handsomest and sweetest and best ladies in the world, and this is the place where freedoms reigns. The bright Bow-of-Promise circles above, and crowns all with a halo of glory; because it is the Land of the Free; and home of the brave. True Patriots all each other greet and hail with joy the sweet song of Liberty.

"Land where my father died,
Land of the Pilgrim's pride,
From every mountain side
Let Freedom ring!!"
My country, my home and my native land.

In the beginning God said, "Let there be light, and there was light. The immortal signers of that glorious declaration on the 4th of July 1776; breathed the spirit of that light. That light was the light of Liberty, which illumines the soul, awakens understanding, opens up a window in Heaven, and says to all "Look up and live." It is that light which marks the triumph of progress which is kindled in every breast, and makes us men indeed.

This light had taken deep root in the Great-American-Start, previous to the Revolution. And when those immortal words were announced to the world; it was a Divinity that marked their utterance.

"When Freedom from her mountain height,
Unfurled her standard in the air;
She decked, the azure robes of night
And set the Stars of Glory there.

The grand epoch in American history was the announcement of those principles of eternal right, by the Old Continental Congress, through Thomas Jefferson "All men are endowed with certain inalienable rights, to wit, Life, Liberty, and the pursuit of Happiness." This is the grand legacy bequeathed to man from the dawn of creation. It is God's law and eternal as the hills.

It was for the faithful perseverance of this great principal that engaged our fore-fathers in the grand struggle for life, liberty, and independence.

The Star of Hope gilded the horizon with festoons of liberty waving in the sunbeams which fired their hearts with holy zeal to strike for the rights of man, Liberty, and their beloved country. The great lights of that day enlisted for life. They were none of your weak-kneed nor feeble-minded who bow at the behest of Tyrant and kiss the hand that is raised to smite them; but, men who were willing to do, and dare; men who staked their all on their country's cause; and offered their lives, a willing sacrifice in vindication of the sacred trust.

A Jefferson, an Adams, a Hancock, a Henry, a Payne, and all the signers of that immortal declaration standing with heads uncovered in the presence of Heaven and the sunlight of truth beaming from their countenance said "We as a light out to be; and shall be free. For God is with us, truth is on our side, then who can stand against us.

Heaven smiled when they signed the grand old parchment. The goddess of liberty hovered over the continental army; and shed tears of grace over a struggling people who had put on the whole armour of truth contending for the rights of man.

After a terrible struggle for seven long years, with a seemingly all-powerful foe, victory perched on the stand and of Liberty. And such a shout went up; "Glory to God in the highest, peace on earth and good will to men" was echoed from every tongue; brave men wept for joy. We had gained the pearl of greatest price. That which places man far above the Brute Creation; midway from nothing to the Deity. We had vindicated our faith on the field of battle. Our success was the triumph of Liberty over a Despotism. We had it written in the blood of our martyred citizens, and proven to the world that Liberty was the dearest and richest treasure that ever was given to man; and that God the great source of light, life and love was on our side. Though truth crushed and bleeding would rise and rule; sovereign, in the ascendant.

All civilized nations of the globe stood in abject wonder, and astonishment, at the magnitude, grandeur, and glory of our success. The love of Liberty had kindled a blaze that could not be put out. That great principle "The right to life, liberty, and the pursuit of happiness" began to move and swell and surge among the people of the Old World. They felt, and heard, and saw the triumph of Liberty in the New. They saw that Little Band of Patriots who had staked all on their country's cause had gained the great reward, and were now rejoicing with joy unspeakable in the broad, bright sunlight of Liberty. The Beacon fires of Liberty were kindled on every hill, and blazing from every hearth stone. The swarming of millions of the Old World saw the light, felt the fires of Liberty kindling in their own hearts set sail for the New. Rejoice O my soul. Let everything that hath breath join in the general jubilee. Blaze on thou glorious light until all nations, peoples and tongues shall come to a full knowledge of the rights of man; and joy and rejoice in the universe sunlight of Freedom.

The Tree of Liberty has taken deep root in the great American heart. Under its wide spreading branches repose all of her sons and daughters. Millions of mortals beyond the big waters look with longing hearts beating with intense emotion, and without stretched arms to the Land of Liberty.

'Tis here the monuments of freedom stand recorded in the Temple of Justice, "Whose spires reach to the very Heavens; and the pillars of Divine Glory descending from God rest forever on its summit." This land is a home for the distressed and persecuted of all nations. At this day and age the best blood, and the most intelligent of the Old World come swarming to the shore of our beloved country. This is a Heaven-favored land; because it is the home of the free. A land of unsurpassed fertility. A land whose broad plains and almost boundless prairies teem with the richest blessings of life to man. A land of free-schools, a free press, and a free people. A land where superstition, bigotry, and religious intolerance have to take a back seat because this is the land where Freedom reigns. The inquisition, the thumb-screw, the frying-pan and guillotine were once the ruling power. But now they are numbered among the things that were. They are only remembered for their brutality and for the ignorance of the age, and the absence of Liberty. It was an age of despotism produced by tyrants - liberty was crushed, reason failed, the voice of suffering humanity appealed in vain. But the star of hope rose in the West. At first it was not larger than a man's hand but soon it spread and the light was seen from far, now its light is seen in every corner of the globe. I see it in this concourse in this great multitude, in this sea of upturned faces. It is the light of liberty beaming from their countenances. That which I see before me today is proof that God is love and that the right to life, liberty and the pursuit of happiness is the inherent right of all mankind.

I see it in your smiling faces, I see it in your laughing eyes, I see it in this mighty crowd. I hear its echo in the boom of cannon, and in the Rolling Drum. I hear it in the multitudinous little voices that have come to swell the general joy by chiming in, on the grand chorus of Liberty, Union, and the rights of man.

This is my country. It is your country. It is our country. It is the "Land of the Free, and Home of the Brave." Shine on Thou glorious land of Liberty; until the whole world shall be filled with the light of thy countenance.

Columbia, the birth-place of Freedom was bought with the blood of our fathers. The mighty conflict opened up on Bunkers Hill, and closed at Yorktown. The God of Battles with a Washington to lead gave us victory, peace, and happiness. And now over Fifty Million rejoice in the sunlight of Freedom.

This great national day; the day of Freedom's birth, is hailed with delight by every true American heart. The watch fire of liberty are blazing from every hill, valley, and plain from the Atlantic to the Pacific. And the Songs of Freedoms triumph are swelling up in tumultuous joy all over the land on this our glorious Independence Day.

Wayside

This light had taken deep root in the Great Amer... previous to the Revolution. And when those words were announced to the world; it was that marked their utterance.

"When Freedom from her mountain height,
Unfurled her standard in the air;
She decked the azure robes of night
And set the Stars of Glory there.

...and epoch in American history was the annu... principles of eternal Right by the Old Continental Cong... Thomas Jefferson "All men are endowed with ma... To wit Life, Liberty, and the pursuit of Happiness... grand legacy bequeathed to man from the dawn of... Gods law, eternal as the hills. No man, thing, ... the moral right to abridge the rights of any on... of those elements which are God given Rights. ... dent free people hold to these rights, which are... As the sun that shines, or the ocean breath... to man. It is Gods law, and eternal as the ... ... for the faithful performance of the ...

…nations of brave blood in astonishment, at the magnitude, grandeur, an…
The love of Liberty ~~It~~ had kindled …
t be put out. That great principle …
nd the pursuit of happiness, began to m…
e among the people of the Old World. The…
the triumph of Libererty in the N…
e Band of Patriots who had staked all…
d gained the great reward, and were…
unspeakable in the broad, bright sun…
on fires of Liberty were kindled on e…
ing from every hearthstone. The su…
Old world saw the Light, felt the…
dling in their own hearts set sail…
my soul. Let everything that hath brea…
al jubilee. Blaze on thou glorious ligh…
peoples and tongues shall come to a full…
hts of man; and few and rejoice in…

sunlight of Freedom.

The Tree of Liberty has taken deep root in American Heart. Under its wide spreading respose all of her sons and Daughters. Millions beyond the big waters look with longing [feel]ing with intense emotion, and with out-stre[tched] to the Land of Liberty.

'Tis here the monuments of Freedom stand recorded i[n] justice, whose spires reach to the very Heavens; [where] of Divine Glory rest forever on its summit. ...

This land is a home for the distressed [children] of all nations. At this day and age the best [and] most intelligent of the Old World come swarmi[ng] of our beloved country.

This is a Heaven-favored land; because it is free. A land of unsurpassed fertility. A lan[d of] plains and almost boundless prairies the richest blessings of life to man. A land of [a] free Religion, and a free people. A land [of free]

our side. Though Truth crushed and bleeding
and rule sovereign, in the ascendant.

All civilized nations of the globe stood in abject
astonishment, at the magnitude, grandeur, and of
Success. The love of Liberty. He had kindled a bla
could not be put out. That great principle Th—
liberty, and the pursuit of happiness, began to mo—
and surge among the people. Old World. They fl—
and saw the triumph of Liberty in the New.
that Little Band of Patriots who had staked all on th—
cause had gained the great reward, and were now
with joy unspeakable in the broad, bright sunligh—
The Beacon fires of Liberty were kindled on every
and blazing from every hearthstone. The swarm—

and surge among the people. Old world. They
and saw the triumph of Liberty in the N—
that Little Band of Patriots who had staked all o—
cause had gained the great reward, and were
with joy unspeakable in the broad, bright sun—
The Beacon fires of Liberty were kindled on e—
and blazing from every hearthstone. The swa—
ions of the Old world saw the Light, felt the
erty kindling in their own hearts set all
Rejoice O my soul. Let everything that hath brea—
the general public. Blaze on thou glorious light
nations, peoples and tongues shall come to a ful—
of the rights of man; and joy and rejoice in

their countenances. That which I see before... (faded handwritten manuscript)

and for the ignorance of the age, and the ab...
It was an age of despotism produced by
was crushed, reason failed, the voice of
manity, appealed in vain. But th...
in the west. At first it was not larger th...
but soon it spread and the light was
Now its light is seen in every corner of
I see it in this concourse, in this great...
Sea of upturned faces. It is the light of l...
their countenances. That which I see before
that God is love and that the right to life,
pursuit of happiness is the inherent right of

...tion, the Thumb-screw, the ...
...ing power and guillotine were f...
But now they are numbered amon...
...re. They are only remembered for their b...
...ance of the age, and the absence of Li...
of despotism produced by Tyrants...
reason failed; the voice of sufferin...
...sealed in vain. But the star of l...
At first it was not larger than a m...
...read and the light was seen fron...

manity appealed in vain
in the west. At first it was not,
but soon it spread and the li...
Now its light is seen in every
I see it in this concourse, in th...
Sea of upturned faces, It is th...
their Countenances. That which I
that God is love and that the rig...
pursuit of happiness is the inheren...

reason failed, the voice of sufferi...
pealed in vain. But the star of
At first it was not larger than a m...
read and the light was seen fro...
t is seen in every corner of the Globe
s concourse, in this great multitude
ned faces, It is the light of liberty bea...
es. That which I see before me to d...
and that the right to life liberty a...
ness is the inherent right of all man...

See it in your smiling faces, See it in
See it in the mighty crowd. I hear its
Cannon, and in the Rolling Drum, I
dinnes little voices that have come to
by chiming in, on the grand chorus
and the rights of man,
This is my country. It is your coun
It is the Land of the Free, and Home of
on Those glorious land of Liberty, u

July
g faces, See him your laughing eyes,
rowd. I hear its echo in the Boom of
ling Drum. I hear it in the Multitu
at have come to swell the general joy
e grand chorus of Liberty, Union,
n,
It is your country. It is our Countr
ee, and Home of the Brave, ,, See
nd of Liberty, until the whole wor

and the rights of man.
This is my Country. It is your country.
It is the Land of the Free; and Home of the B
on Thou glorious land of Liberty; until th
Shall be filled with the light of thy Counte
Columbia, the birth-place of freedom
the blood of our fathers. The mighty conflict
Bunker hill and closed at Yorktown, the
Washington to lead gave us victory, f
piness. And now over fifty million f
Freedom
This great natal Day; the

CHAPTER FOURTEEN

ONLY A TRAMP

BY

WILLIAM MCFARLAND

'WAYSIDE'

A great sensation. "A dead man found beside the railroad 1½ miles this side of Buda Village Thursday morning April 25th 1878. The coroner was called, a jury was impaneled and inquest held. Decision and verdict rendered "accidental."

Supposed to be a case of apoplexy, or, some such disease, no wounds or bruises were found on the body. He doubtless belonged to the gust army of tramps who fill the whole country. He stayed at Buda Village the night before and slept in the Depot. He was heard to say while there that he would as lief die as live as he was out of money and work and not being well was forced to beg, can it be possible? Must people starve to death in this land of plenty? Where is Providence, and where is the Machine? On examination his stomach his stomach was found to be empty. There was water on the brain. It is supposed that when he sat down to rest, his head being dizzy he probably fainted, fell over, and rolled into the ditch; where he smothered to death in the mud and water.

"Only a tramp, shut the door." Nearly every day we read of some poor tramp who has passed in his checks. He is driven from door to door as unworthy of notice; sick and tired, dirty and ragged, with his ambition all gone he sits down anywhere, dirty and ragged, with his ambition all gone he sits down anywhere; cares for nothing; no, not even himself; curses the world in which he was born; looks back to the place of his once happy home; despair gets hold of him, that good old home is gone; those happy days are ended; he banishes home, friends, everything from his thoughts, but his utter loneliness and destitution, and then lies down to rise no more. There is no note or mark to identify him. Here is only a tramp, a poor wandering, worthless tramp; shunned and rejected; refused admission everywhere. He is nothing but a tramp. O! How a poor mother's heart must feel when she reads this notice. My poor boy is away from home, may be sick, and tired, and foot sore tramping from place to place, asking for shelter and food. To have the door shut in his face and to have those dreadful, awful words. "Shut the door, he is only a tramp." The very thought of such would wring many a poor mother's heart. "I was a stranger and ye took me not in; naked and ye took me not; sick, and ye visited me not." "When saw we thee an hungered, or a thirst, or a stranger, or naked, or sick and did not minister unto thee!" Then shall he answer them saying, "Verily, I say unto you as ye did it not to one of the least of these (even this poor tramp) ye did it not to me!" "Depart from me I know you not."

... to death in the mud and water.

x   x   x   x   x   x   x

"Only a tramp, shut the door." Nearly every day a poor tramp who has passed in his check. There is to door so unworthy of notice; sick and tired, dirty and ambition all gone he sits down anywhere; cares for even himself; curses the world in which he ... back to the place of his once happy home; despair gets hold ... old home is gone, those happy days are ended; his friends, everything from his thought but his utter destitution, and then lies down to rise no more ... or mark to identify him. He is only a tramp, a ... worthless tramp; Spurned and rejected; ...

... worthless tramp; Spurned and rejected; everywhere. He is nothing but a tramp. ... ers heart must feel when she reads this ... Boy is away from home, may be sick, ... more tramping from place to place, ... food. To have the door shut in his fa... beautiful awful words." Shut the door, he ... The very thought of such would wring ... ers heart. "I was a stranger and ye took ... me not; sick, and ye visited ...

friend...

destitution, and then lies down to rise no...
or mark to identify him. He is only a...
ings, worthless tramp; spurned and reject...
everywhere. He is nothing but a tramp...
er's heart must feel when she reads th...
Boy is away from home, may be si...
poor tramping from place to place...
foot. To have the door shut in his...
dreadful, awful word "Shut the door,...
The very thought of such would wring...
er's heart. "I was a stranger and ye to...
...not; sick, and ye visited

Not answering, saying "When saw we thee an hungered, or...
or a stranger, or naked, or sick, and did not minister un...
"Then shall he answer them saying "Verily I say unto you...
it not to one of the least of these (even this poor tram) ye di...
me." "Depart from me...

Memorial Day   1877

Washington wept over the fate of Maj. André. Du...
shed tears over the sleeping of Napoleon 1st. But Maj. ...
Hamilton could not permit even one flower to be put on...
of the Confederate dead, and even asked forgiveness fo...
one year ago. His hate is so intense — his charity so s...
his love of party exceeds his love for humanity. ...

CHAPTER FIFTEEN

MEMORIAL DAY 1879

BY

WILLIAM MCFARLAND

'WAYSIDE'

Washington wept over the fate of Maj. Amitri. Queen Victoria shed tears over the sleeping of Napoleon 1st. But Maj. Gent Hamilton could not permit even one flower to be put over the graves of the confederate dead, and even asked forgiveness for allowing it one year ago. His hate is so intense - his charity so small; that his love of party exceeds his love of humanity. All the carpet boy thieves seem to stand higher in his estimations than the honest rebel dead. The orator of the day May 30/78 Rev. at Kewanee Lake seemed to travel in the same rut, and Gov. at Jollietville was given in the same measure. Col. at Princeton Lake was some better; there was less rancor and hate manifested, but still partisan seemed to linger in the folds of the Honorables speech which would chill the blood of many war Democrats. He can't be of that narrow hearted, self conceited, God and morality party that loves to hate. Such words return to curse the inventor, such words are unworthy of a noble and generous heart. A party that cannot show due courtesy to a dead foe, or generous erring brother is unworthy of the intelligent living. All honest patriots everywhere have reconnect for a brave for who lost his life in battle especially if he was contending for what he thought was right. Answer then can't do this is full worthy of the respect of the intelligent living. Can the Republican party be like generous than the Queen of the greatest nations on earth (Victoria). Can we as Americans forget that we have a Washington who shed tears over a fallen foe? Can we as independent free men still cherish hate towards a dead erring brother who forfeiture his life contending for what he supposed to be right? This cold inveterate will certainly destroy you. Where is that grand old party today? That grand old party whose word was power and whose will was law? Does she not now lie strangling within the evils of her own wearing? Her days are numbered. She has been weighed in a balance and found war.

cannot show due courtesy to a dead,
is unworthy of the intelligent living.

for a brave foe ... his life in bat[tle]
ing for what he thought was right ...
generous than the Queen of the greates[t]
Can we as americans forget that ...
shed tears over a fallen foe? Can w[e]
still cherish hate towards a deade[r]
his life contending for what he supp[osed]
inveterate will certainly destroy ...

CHAPTER SIXTEEN

THE BIG FOUR
PLUS ONE
BY
WILLIAM MCFARLAND
'WAYSIDE'

The Barber is the grand emporium of knowledge. What he doesn't know isn't worth talking about. His verbosity and loquacity is proverbial. He can start any time, talk all the time and never say anything but will leave your mind as much in the dark at the ending as it was at the beginning. He is a kind-hearted, good, clever fellow; chock full of the milk of human kindness, lofty expressions and generous to a fault. He always looks slick and clean. He is the grand central figure of all parties, dances, shin-digs. If it was not for the barber, the world would cease to be what it is, and mankind would fairly rust out of existence. He is necessary to all trades and professions. He dresses the parson's wig, polishes the gentleman's boots and shoes, gives the finishing twist to the dandy's moustache, adds grace and beauty to the ladies curls and gives color to the light on the upper lip of young America. O! Who wouldn't be a barber and shine forever-more.

The next in order is the village blacksmith; a man of giant mold, Herculean frame, and thoroughly posted on horse-heaven. He is a true believer in the signs of the times, and knows everybody. He is very fond of joking and when tickled laughs all over. The blacksmith is no hypocrite but can look as sanctimonious on Sunday at church as a deacon. He is very fond of loud singing, but does not like the Machine. He is a firm believer in the scriptures and in Heaven and Hell, but is doubtful on utility of brimstone except in extreme cases. He holds to inspiration. Believes that preachers have a call from above. But often thinks that Providence is imposed upon by some men calling themselves. Doubts the philosophy of revolving worlds. Believes that the earth is flat and stand still while the sun moves; because Joshua told the sun to stand still. Sure would not have told it to stand still if it was not moving.

The Jolly Shoemaker is the happiest man alive. He is a regular journeyman sole saver; merry as a lark and happy as a clam. He never frets in the harness; but, believes in enjoying the good things of this world while he can and take a little of the O be joyful for his stomach sake. Believes that a stitch in time will save a dime; plays Euchre, Old-Sledge, Dominoes and whisky poker for the drinks. When he is out he is as spry as a cat. Takes a race to the coal shaft every day and always wins. He is no tee-to-teller but swallows his whisky straight. When you wish to see a jolly happy crowd, just get among a lot of inflated shoemakers. They are very fond of the fair sex, but will never insult a lady but will fight for one at the drop of a hat.

Our Deacon is a model of perfection and as straight as a cork-screw. He is strong in the faith, mighty in prayer and when he stamps his foot things have to tumble. He is a strong temperance man. Will neither touch, taste nor handle not the unclean thing! No, never! Only as a medicine, or when his liver is out of order. He is willing to have all men damned for Christ sake except himself. He is a Tyrant at home but a saint in the church. He is so holy that butter wouldn't melt in his mouth in dog-days. He sits at the head of the Amen Choir and respond to the echo. The Deacon has looked solemn so long that his fate grows crooked whenever he attempts to smile.

Our squire is a portly good looking old fellow; the true type of the fine old English gentleman. Good natured, takes things as he finds them and never frets in the harness. Has plenty, lives easy, and takes his whisky straight. Is very charitable and spends his money freely. Has no poor relations and never goes in debt. Believes in free trade and sailor's rights, but always patronizes home industry by taking the Tribune. He is no infidel, but hates hypocrisy; favors not the mangling of church and state but that everything should stand on its own merits. Don't bother himself about a future state but takes the world as he finds it. He is not very particular about his inheritance in Glory World. But is willing to take most any good locations not situated too far from the brewery.

Wayside

...tion. O! who wouldn't be a ...
...more.

...he village Blacksmith; a man of
...n frame, and thoroughly posted on
...is a true believer in the signs of the
... body. He is very fond of joking and
...all over. The Blacksmith is no less
...s sanctimonious on Sunday at church
...very fond of clound singing, but does
...He is a firm believer in the scriptures
...Hell, but is doubtful on utility of
...extreme cases. He holds to inspiration
... have a call from above. But often
...is imposed upon by some mere call
...s the philosophy of revolving worlds
...th is flat and stand still while the
...se Joshua told the sun to stand
... have told it to stand still if it

146

The Big Tree plan, One

but took the world as he finds it. He is not very particular
about his inheritance in Glory World. But is willing to
... any good location not too far from the
Brewery

What is Christianity?

What is Christianity? And what is the religion of the Bible?
I used to believe yet when I was a boy, that the religion of ...
... it was above every earthly consideration; that its value could
... be weighed or measured. But this is a progressive age,
... have greatly changed. Temperance takes the lead now. ...
... can have agreed congregation except on Temperance ni...
... this? Is prohibition of greater value or superior to C...
...? Or has the old version played out? We know that
most eminent Divines said that Christianity was not ...
... to make a good radical Temperance man ... Man...
... of our churches on temperance night reveals this fact; the
... unbelievers and even Atheists are permitted to teach
... of the fullest even scoffers of religion are given a ...
... This is an age of progress and mankind is the wi...
... Christianity and the Bible have had a birth ...
... new fangled steps of Prohibition, truly called Temperan...
... in temperance, and intend to live and die a ...

CHAPTER SEVENTEEN

FERGUSON

BY

WILLIAM McFARLAND

'WAYSIDE'

A thousand times ten thousand years have rolled this ample rounds since first the great universe of God's creation was in its infancy. The silent fields of the long unknown and dead past rises before me. Who can measure the heights and depths of God's creation, or tell when the beginning of matter was?

The thought's too great for mortal man,

Let all try who will

Nothing but God, and God alone,

Infinite space can fill.

Neponset City has been stirred from centre to circumference by one of the grandest intellectual feasts ever given to man; almost beyond belief or comprehension; such a grand display of the dark and dreamy past, enfolded and brought to light by one whose very vocabulary bespeaks a genius of the first magnitude, beamed upon us with his most refulgent rays.

Mr. Ferguson of Cattonsville, who has long been employed in scientific researches for the government, the transit of planets, the astronomical of the solar system and the geology of the earth gave us a series of lectures during last week on the above topics, captivating everybody who heard him, and causing many to attend church who never went there before. Such a fine display of dreamy dead past has been rarely equaled. Such an inexhaustible fund of acquired knowledge in one man seems almost impossible. This grand magnet of attraction turned all eyes towards the sidereal heavens. Then taking all by the seat of their inexpressible he carries them off into the great fields of illimitable space and there feast on the rich luxuries and ripe fruit of the empty real vineyards of Jupiter, Saturn, Uranus and Neptune and revel with unbounded delight on the tablet of the sunbeams. Never before has Neponset City had such a grand ride. Science opened the way and genius under control of a master mind, romped and played with the sun, moon and fixed stars as if they were toys or titular dignitaries of the chess-board. Space was annihilated. The subterranean depths of the dreamy past were brought to light.

The grand pageant of revolving worlds long before the creation of Adam passed in quick review before our astonished vision. Then like a flush of thought he mounts above the Milky Way. Basks in the region of the fixed stars, pluck fresh laurels from the farthest planet and drinks in the rich, deep moisture that flows from their crystal fountains. Then, after being filled with a full knowledge of the upper deep returns to wander among the sons and daughters of men. He is truly a wonderful man, whose very reach of thoughts proclaims the soul immortal. One whose quickened mind reaches far beyond the things of time and sense. One who mounts on wings of living light to Eden's highest plains and shines along the Grand Boulevard of the Great Eternal.

Prof. Ferguson lectured here every night last week in this place to a well filled house closing with a perfect avalanche on Sunday night. By contrast he lectures in Kewanee Lake all this week. It will pay one to hear him.

Wayside

Ferguson

thousand times in a thousand years have
since first the great universe of God's ere
the fields of the long unknown and dee
to measure the heights and depths a
the beginning of matter was?
The thoughts too great for mortal mi
Let all try who will

the geology of the earth gave us a series of
week on the above topics, captivating eve
and causing many to attend church wh
Such a fine display of the dreamy dead
equalled, Such an inexhaustible fund
in one man seems almost impossible. I
attraction turned all eyes towards the Sidere
king all by the seal of their inexpressibles he
the great fields of Illimitable space and there
one ripe fruit of the Empyreal Vineyards
Uranus and Neptune and revel with un
the tablet of the Sunbeams. Never before befo

of a hat.

Our Deacon is a model of perfection and is a cork screw. He is strong in the faith, and when he stamps his foot things have He is a strong temperance man will ne ver handle out the unclean thing, no, a medicine, or when his liver is out He is willing to have all men damned except himself He is a tyrant at h in the church, He is so holy that butter in his mouth in dog days. He sits at Amen Chead and response to the echo

Bird catches the worm. But I am the a plenty of sleep, and I will grow, and get fat get my nap out, I won't be cross and ugly much better it is to wake up with a smile on own. All young people require a good dea uld go to bed early, so as to get their nap out rious to health, as to rob youth of its required p and undisturbed rest, is best for soul and d boys romp and play, until tired nature play while the sunshines. But when night t comfortable little bed that Ma has made for Cot so snug, so neat and clean. Then close

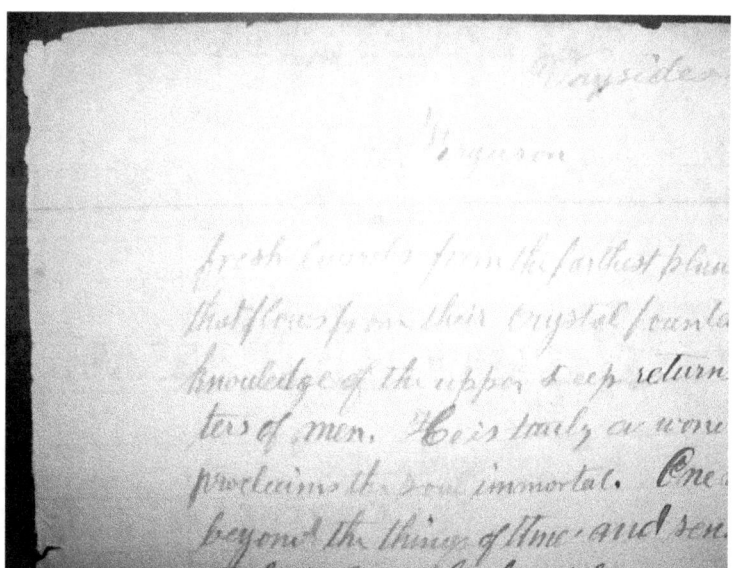

PART TWO

Silence In Heaven

And The Butter-Woman

Wayside Stories

By

William McFarland

Wayside

Worm Of The Still

By

William McFarland

'Wayside'

1.

There came to my door a heart broken stranger;

The dew on his thin robe was heavy and chill;

He cried I am ruin'd, my life is in danger,

By that dreadful monster "The Worm of Still"

O! Cruel wilt thou never release me,

And give wings to fly where no peril can chase me;

Away from this monster, where he never can find me;

Away from this Serpent "The Worm of the Still."

2.

I've wander'd away from my once lovely dwelling;
Where joys bright and pure my moments did fill;
But, Alas! They have vanish'd while Satan was filling
My soul with a poison; the drugs of the Still.
O! Give me respite for one happy hour!
One hour of rest from this dread Destroyer,
One hour of peace untainted by sorrow,
The peace that comes not from "The Worm of the Still"
Thy peace that comes not from "The Worm of the Still."

3.

My life is fast sinking, my sun is descending;
Already dark chains encompass my will;
I feel the torments of pain never ending;
Brought on by that monster "The Worm of Still"
My dear loving partner has pass'd o'er the river;
My two little darlings gone, gone forever;
Now resting in Heaven with Jesus their Savior
And I left a slave to the "Worm of the Still"

4.

O friends won't you help me Look! There! See him coming!
His eyes blaze like fireballs, He'll have me! He will!
O save me from Satan, the Son of Perdition!
The source of all evil! "The Worm of the Still"
I stretch'd out my arms and pointed to Heaven,
Though your sins be like mountains may all be forgiven;
Made pure bright and holy in God's blissful Eden;
Secure from that monster, the Worm of the Still.

Wayside

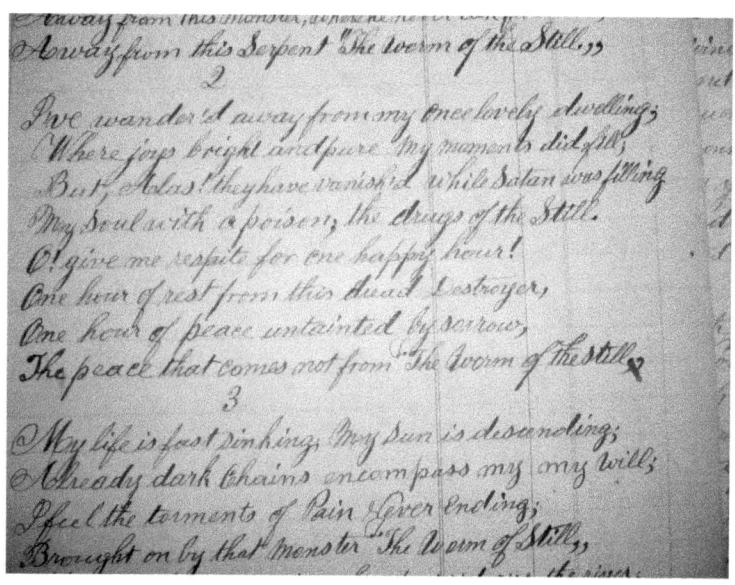

...our of peace untainted by sorrow,
The peace that comes not from "The Worm of the...

3

My life is fast sinking, My sun is descende...
Already dark Chains encompass my m...
I feel the torments of Pain & ever ending;
Brought on by that Monster "The Worm of Still...
My Dear loving partner has pass'd over th...
My two little Darlings gone— gone forever,
Now resting in Heaven with Jesus their S...
And I left a slave to the "Worm of the Sti...

4

O friends wont you help me Look! There! ...
his eyes blaz like fire balls, He'l have m...
Save me from Satan, the Son of Perd...
the Source of all evil!" "The Worm of...
reatch'd out my arms and pointed t...
ugh your sins be like Mountains may...
de pure bright and Holy in Gods ...
ure from that Monster, the Worm ...

3

My life is fast sinking; My Sun is a[lready]
Already dark [chains] encompass [me]
I feel the torments of Pain & Fever [end]
Brought on by that Monster "The Worm[
My Dear loving partner has pass'd [away]
My two little Darlings gone — gone for[
Now resting in Heaven with Jesus [
And I left a slave to the "Worm of [death]

And I left a slave to the worm of [death]

4

O friends wont you help me Look! The[re]
His eyes blaze like fire balls, He'll hav[e]
Save me from Satan, the Son of P[erdition]
The Source of all evil! "The Worm[
I streatch'd out my arms and pointe[d]
Though your sins be like mountains ma[y be]
Made pure bright and Holy in God[
Secure from that monster, the Worm

me Look! There! See him coming!
lls, He'l have me! He will!
the Son of Perdition!
"The Worm of the Still,
and pointed to Heaven;
untains may all be forgiven;
Holy in Gods Blissful Eden;
ter, the Worm of the Still Ways

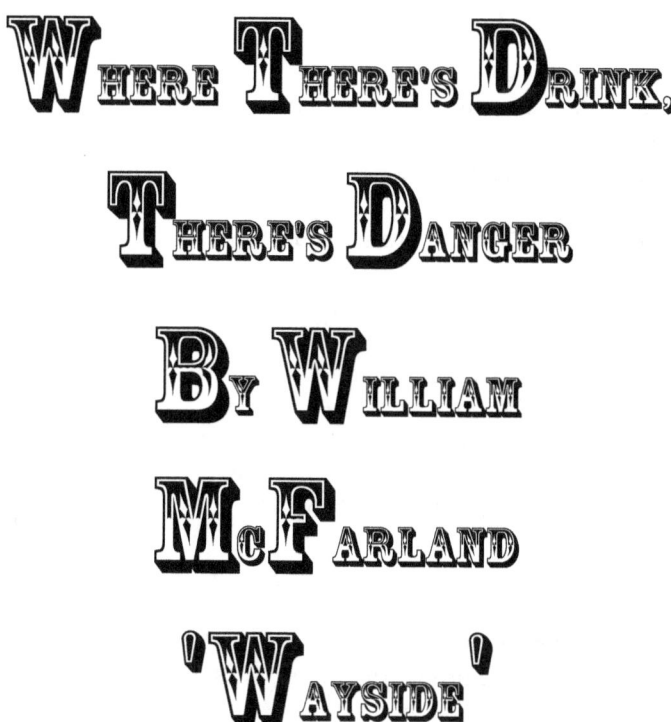

Where There's Drink, There's Danger
By William McFarland
'Wayside'

1.

Write it on the liquor store, Where there's drink,
Write it on the prison door, Where there's drink,
Write it on the gin-shop sign, Where there's drink,
In plainest words this truthful line, Where there's drink,
Where there's Drink, there's Danger!

2.

Write it on the work-shop gate,
Write it on the school-boy's slate,
Write it on each copy-book,
So each child, may on it look,
Where there's Drink, there's Danger!

3.

Write it on each church yard mound,
Where the drink-slain dead are found,
Write it on the gallows high;
Write it for all passersby;
Where there's Drink, there's Danger!

4.

Write it underneath your feet -
Up and down the busy street, -
Write it for the great and small -
In the mansion, cot, and hall -
Where there's Drink, there's Danger!

5.

Write it in the Christian's home,
Write it where the drunkards roam,
Year by year from God and right,
Proving with unerring sight,
Where there's Drink, there's Danger!

6.

Write it on the verdant page,
Write it, patriot, scholar, sage,
Write it in the Sabbath School,
Write it plain the truth and rule,
Where there's Drink, there's Danger!

7.

Write it on the House of God;
Write it on the teeming sod;
Write it on the hilltop, glen,
Write it for all sons of men,
Where there's Drink, there's Danger!

8.

Write it for the rising youth,

Write it for the cause of truth,

Write, it for My Father Land,

Write, 'tis Duty's stern command,

Where there's Drink there's Danger.

9.

Write it for Bright Heaven above,

Write it for the God of love;

Write it near the fire-side;

And for Christ who for man died,

Where there's Drink there's Danger.

Write it on the Work-shop Gate,
Write it on the School-Boy's Slate,
Write it on each copy Book.
So ~~that~~ each Child may on it look.

                    Where there's Drink

3

Write it on each Church-Yard m
Where the Drink-Slain-Dead are fo
Write it on the Gallows high;
Write it for all passers by;

the Work-shop Gate,
he School-Boy's Slate,
ach copy Book.
Child may on it look,

            Where there's Drink, there's Danger!

3

n each Church-Yard mound,
Drink-Slain-Dead are found,
the Gallows high;
all passers by;

            Where there's Drink there's Danger!

4

Write it underneath your feet
Up and down the busy street
Write it for the Great and Small
In the Mansion, Cot, and Hall
Where there's Drink there

5

Write it in the Christians Home,
Write it where the Drunkards roam
Year by year from God and Right
... with unerring Sight

6

Where there's Drink there's Danger

7

Write it in the House of God;
Write it on the teeming Sod;
Write it on the hilltop, Glen,
Write it for all sons of men
Where there's Drink there's Dang

8

In Memoriam

By

William McFarland

'Wayside'

Dead at last, and gone to rest

In yonder grave-yard on the hill;

He lies beneath the clover sod,

Waiting there his master's will.

Silence In Heaven And The Butter-Woman And Other
Wayside Stories
by Wayside

Dead at last, no friends to mourn,

No one to drop a fallen tear.

No father's voice, no mother's care,

No brother, sister, - not one near.

Died at last and gone to rest;

His toils and troubles all are o'er;

Passed over Jourdan's stormy blast,

To wait 'till time shall be no more.

Gems Of The Quill

By

William McFarland

'Wayside'

Silence In Heaven And The Butter-Woman And Other
Wayside Stories
by Wayside

1.

Fellow friends of the quill in compliments kind,
You're ever before me embalmed in my mind;
Behold in bright vision I see far away,
On the ever-green shore,
It gives me great pleasure, in sunshine, or rain,
To meet and converse with my friends once again;
And feast on gems of love and good-will;
Together rejoice with friends of the quill.

2.

O who can measure the worth of the pen;
The value deriv'd, bestowed upon men;
The puissant quill that ever doth flow,
A river of life to all here below.
With high swelling sail how gaily we glide
On the waves of this reportorial tide;
'Tis the life of the soul. It makes the heart thrill,
And throb with delight, those "Gems of the Quill."

3.

The birds of the grove in concert do sing;
Chirrup and flutter, and sail on the wing.
They gather in circles and then when away,
In chorus of song the smiles of the day.
The printers and people come at the call
To grace the occasion and roll on the ball;
Their presence and greetings show their good-will,
And, heightens the joys with the "Gems of the Quill."

4.

The balm of the soul, the blessings of life,
Is taught by the quill, and found in a wife;
They ever stand ready with body and soul,
To drive away sorrow and make the heart whole
The ladies God bless! We ever do find
Them friends to reporters; the very best kind,
They give us a feast of love and good-will
Well flavor'd with spice and "Gems of the Quill."

5.

Go gather in gold and try if you can
The pleasure of wealth to make happy man
No solace there find, no, not one in ten
To equal the Quill. The good little pen.
There's nothing on earth - can't find any-where
An equal to this reportorial fare;
'Tis made of the best with delicate skill;
And flavor'd with spice from Gems of the Quill.

6.

'Tis full nutrition develops the mind;
Gives virtue a flavor so delicate, kind;
It unravels thought and opens the eyes,
And learns people every-where how to be wise,
Go travel abroad over land over sea;
And gather in him of all company;
The good and the wise and all great the toper
Your company's slim without a reporter

7.

This fountain is full and never runs dry;
Nor never was known to fail in supply;
He walks in the light and ever doth rove
Through flowers of thought and bouquets of love.
He is more potent when time's on the wing,
Than Marquis or Duke, or Monarch, or King.
The very best seat which no one can fill,
Is kept in reserve for one of the Quill.

8.

His pen's on the wing as upward he flies,
To gather fresh laurels and gems from the skies;
The sweetest of verse to us he will bring,
And gladden all hearts with songs of the spring,
This jewell's or treasure, it never gets old;
Far better than wealth and brighter than gold.
His home is on high, it rests there at will,
And lights the whole with Gems of the Quill.

9.

A very swift witness to shew us the evil
Of cravings desire, the flesh and the Devil;
Is thoroughly posted and knows how to dock it,
When men make a corner, and sell out of pocket.
He scans the broad plain where bargains are made;
Diverges the cunning of all Boards of Trade;
Is faithful and true and ever doth fill,
The grand post of honor with "Gems of the Quill."

10.

A genial soul, so nimble and spry;
Is alive and awake to all passing by;
He spreads a repast delicious and stable;
Enough, and for all, a bountiful table.
Has news there abundant the richest in store;
And ever stands waiting to gather some more;
Gives freedom to thought the birth-right of will,
The feast of the soul from "Gems of the Quill."

11.

Here the proud Banner of Freedom's unfurled
Giving joy to the heart and light to the world;
We join in the chorus and chant to its roll,
The freedom of thought and flow of the soul.
'Tis knowledge that speaks commands us to act;
Rejoices the whole in giving the fact;
There's nothing on earth their mission can fill,
And cause light to sparkle like "Gems of the Quill."

12.

As time rolls along we run to and fro,
And gather fresh light wherever we go;
The freedom of thought presented to view,
Enlivens the soul with things that are new.
The scope of the soul is wide in its range;
To those of small minds does seem very strange;
They understand not the powers of will,
When truth's made to sparkle from Gems of the Quill.

13.

The reporter's pen it runs like a dream,
Is held by the wise in highest esteem;
With delicate touches he treats all your views,
And pleases the world by giving news.
They shine in the parlors of grandest estate;
And dine with the wise, the good, and the great;
Their lamps shines a far, it stands on a hill;
And lighted by gas from "Gems of the Quill."

14.

Sometimes we may err, sometimes go astray;
For its uphill and down along the whole way;
Sometimes we have plenty, sometimes not a grain
But that is all luck we'll try it again.
The progress of light develops the truth;
Gives wisdom to age, inspires the youth;
I see a long line that's marching up hill;
That walk in the light from "Gems of the Quill."

15.

Though pleasure and pain unceasingly flow
All through the wide world wherever we go;
Yet joy fills the heart to think of that day
When we shall report in the Grand Faraway.
I gaze in sweet rapture. I see the bright shore,
Where life everlasting shall bloom evermore;
I hear the loud anthems the musical thrill,
As echoed in song by Gems of the Quill.

16.

Undying thought triumphant doth sail
O'er fathomless deeps the mystical vale;
It opens the heart inspires with love
And points with delight to Bowers above.
I see the Grand Army that's moving along;
That mingle their voices in chorus of song;
I read in the Bible our Father's good-will,
Who gave us the light from Gems of the Quill.

17.

Then Hail to the light since time it began;
The greatest of blessings bestow'd upon man;
The life of the soul, of earth and of air,
Recorded in light by the pen everywhere.
Then blow gentle gales and fill every breeze,
With odors of incense blossoming trees,
Bid thunders to roll o'er valley and hill
And echo the song, "The Gems of the Quill."

18.

The light of the soul is fading away;
And soon with the earth will crumble its clay;
Yet hope springs aloft, the Lord will provide
From Gems of the Quill another "Wayside"
My sun's fast sinking down low in the West,
From labor and toil the night giveth rest;
Yet while life shall last there's nothing can thrill,
Or, warm up the heart like Gems of the Quill.

Wayside

Together rejoice with friends of the Quill

2

O who can measure the worth of the Pen;
The value deriv'd,— bestow'd upon men;
The puissant Quill that ever doth flow,
A river of life to all here below.
With high swelling sail how gaily we glide
On the waves of this reportorial tide;
'Tis the life of the soul. It makes the heart thrill,
And throb with delight; those "Gems of the Q

3

The birds of the grove in concert do sing;
Chirrup and flutter and sail on the wing.

'Tis the life of the soul. It makes the heart thrill,
And throb with delight; those "Gems of the Quill,"

3

The birds of the grove in concert do sing;
Chirrup and flutter and sail on the wing.
They gather in circles and then whir away,
In chorus of song the smiles of the day.
The printers and people come at the call
To grace the occasion and roll on the ball;
Their presence and greetings show their Good will,
And hightens the joys. Sing "Gems of the Quill"

4

The Balm of the soul— The Blessings of life,
Is taught by the Quill, and found in a wife
and with body and soul

'Tis full nutrition develops the mind
Gives virtue a flavor so delicate, kind
It unravels thought and opens the eyes
And learns people everywhere how to
To travel abroad, overland, over
Together in kind of all Company
The good and the wise, great and the
Your Company's slim without a

6

7

The good and the wise

Your Company's slim without a reporter

7

This fountain is full and never runs dry
Nor never was known to fail in supply
He walks in the light and ever doth rev
Through flowers of thought and Bouquets
He is more potent when time's on the w
Than Marquis or Duke, or Monarch, or K
The very best seat which no one can fill
Is kept in reserve for one of the Quill

8

Gems of Quill continued

9

A very swift witness to shew us the er...
Of craving Desire, the Flesh and the Dev...
thoroughly posted and knows how to de...
When men make a term, and sell out of pocke...
Scans the broad plain where bargains a...
Divulges the Cunning of all Boards of Tra...
faithful and true and ever doth fill
...grand post of honor with "Gems of the Q...

The grand post of honor with "Gems of the Quill,"

10

A genial soul, so nimble and spry;
B alive and awake to all passing by;
He spreads a repast delicious and stable;
Enough, and for all, a bountiful table.
Has news there abundant the richest in store,
And ever stands waiting to gather some more;
Gives freedom to thought the birth-right of will,
The feast of the soul from "Gems of the Quill"

11

Here the proud Banner of Freedom's unfur...

The feast of the Soul from "Gems of the Quill,"

11

Here the proud Banner of Freedom's unfur
Giving Joy to the heart and light to the wo
We join in the Chorus and Chant to its roo
The freedom of thought and flow of the sou
'Tis knowledge that speaks commands us t
Rejoices the whole in giving the fact;
There's nothing on earth their mission ca
And cause light to sparkle like "Gems of

12

As time rolls along we run to and fro,

Gems of the Quill

17

Then Hail to the light since time it began;
The greatest of blessings bestowed upon man;
The life of the soul, of earth and of air,
Recorded in light by the pen everywhere.
Then blow gentle gales and fill every breeze,
With odors of incense Blossoming trees,
Bid thunders to roll o'er valley and hill
And echo the song "The Gems of the Quill.

18

The light of the soul is fading away;
And soon with the earth will crumble its clay;
Yet Hope springs aloft, The Lord will provide
From Gems of the Quill another "Wayside,
My sun's fast sinking down low in the west,
From labor and toil the night giveth rest;
Yet while life shall last there's nothing can th
Or, warm up the heart like Gems of the Quill.

Actual handwriting of Wayside with his pen name on it
and thus this is like his autograph!

Photo taken of the actual old book cover with some of the very old, antique pages still inside. This is the very same book cover that protected these writings for over 123 years. I separated its pages and sorted them and have made several books out of its contents.

THE END

Silence In Heaven And The Butter-Woman And Other
Wayside Stories
by Wayside